From Destinations Set

Christopher Nosnibor

From Destinations Set

Christopher Nosnibor

2011
Clinicality Press
York, England

From Destinations Set
Copyright © 2010 Clinicality Press

First published 2010 by Clinicality Press
First paperback edition 2011
http://clinicalitypress.co.uk

ISBN 978-0-9556939-6-0

It was just another day at the office, the same as any other. Tim sat at his desk. He had spent the last three hours trying desperately to compile his latest report based on a series of site visits to out-of-town shopping developments ahead of Friday's deadline, but it was proving nigh on impossible. For a start, the buildings were in a poor state of repair: his surveys had uncovered a number of significant structural flaws which were bad news all round. The trouble was, he found these modern prefabricated monstrosities composed of concrete and corrugated iron the most uninspiring of all buildings to assess, and while he had most of the information he required to hand, some of his notes were a little patchy regarding some of the sites, as he had been tired, bored and hungover while conducting the surveys. That said, he didn't really find buildings in themselves all that inspiring. Surveying hadn't been a calling for him, but then, for whom is surveying a calling, a passion? Surveying was a job, which required an even and pragmatic approach to factual data and a grasp of figures and certain scientific concepts regarding the deterioration of concrete, the weakening of iron girders, the flammability of certain

It's no easy task being a writer. I certainly don't believe one 'chooses' to be a writer – I shan't say 'become' a writer, because the word has implications of evolution. That isn't to say that a writer doesn't evolve or grow – writing requires a great deal of practice and commitment – but a writer doesn't start as something else and then slowly turn into a writer. No, a writer starts out as a writer, and then develops with time, practice and experience. Well, so one would hope, and I'm quite certain that my own output now is almost infinitely better than it was fifteen years ago. But I'd still say I was a writer then. I didn't choose to write. It was a compulsion. Same as it is now.

But today my compulsion seems compelled to pursue other things...

Ant Barker had been staring at the screen for what seemed like hours. He checked the clock on his Microsoft® Windows© XP desktop. He had been staring at the screen for hours. The text was beginning to drift before his eyes as he read it again and again. His narrative was increasingly turning to opinion and editorial. He didn't consider this a problem per se, but he had ground to a halt mid-paragraph as he wondered if he had not wandered a little too far off track and

materials and so on. The appreciation of architecture was not a prerequisite for becoming a surveyor of commercial property. But the modern out-of-town retail park developments were still the worst: once you had seen one, you had seen them all. But feeling tired and grotty made any report on such buildings even more wearisome, and with a tight deadline looming, even more troublesome to a man who was not a big fan of typing long reports, preferring, if possible, to keep communications down to brief notes and bullet-points. Equally troublesome, his phones – landline and mobile – kept ringing, interfering with his train of thought. No sooner had he regained his flow and begun formulating a coherent sentence detailing the defects in the roofing structures or damp coursing than another call would demand his attention and haul him away from the job at hand for just long enough for him to forget exactly what it was he had been about to write next. Tim sat and rubbed his eyes with his thumb and forefinger. His skin felt rough and dry, his eyes sensitive and watery. He was exhausted, and this was reflected in his sallow appearance. He had spent the last week and a half driving long-distance between the sites he was surveying for this report –

simply written about himself at that moment in time. Was he writing a character or was he simply writing himself? He paused to think. There was, to his mind, no point in writing for the sake of it, to produce screes of inferior prose only to delete them again later. He was a writer with a conscience, and also a burning desire to change things.

It was his objective to write the world: he wanted to right the world. Ultimately, he wanted to rewrite the world. The process would be long and arduous. There was no simple or direct route. As he saw it, to write the world, one must live in the world. Then, one must record and exorcise, commit to paper all of the horrors, the ugliness, the hatred, the sickness, record the sights and the smells and the sounds in all of their repulsive vileness. To write the world is to run through the pain and anguish of living, and the writing process requires the reliving of it all, in its entirety, experiencing once more the agony and suffering, only this time with a greater intensity than the first time, than of the actual event, in order to distil it all and encapsulate it – not simply to capture, but to intensify in order to convey with the same intensity through a neutral medium. Potency is otherwise lost in transmission. The

Wednesday last: Sheffield, Thursday last: Birmingham, Friday last: Nottingham; followed by Bath on Monday; Stoke on Tuesday; Newcastle on Wednesday and Norwich this morning – before returning to the office with a sheaf of scribbled notes, digital camera shots, notes recorded on a Dictaphone while on the tops of various buildings, muffled and inaudible due to high winds blasting across the mic as he had mumbled tiredly and unenthusiastically about various joists and joints.

He rubbed his eyes again and returned his bleary pupils to the screen. He had been staring at the screen for what felt like hours. How long it had really been, he was uncertain. The text was beginning to drift before his eyes as he read it again and again. The text was beginning to drift before his eyes as he read it again and again. The text was beginning to drift before his eyes as he read it again and again. The text was beginning to drift before his eyes as he read it again and again. The text was beginning to drift before his eyes

He needed a break. Needed to clear his head, to regain his focus. Yes, he had a deadline looming, but he'd never make it like this. Just a few minutes of doing something – anything – to take his mind off the task at hand

page, the ink, will not leap out and physically batter the reader with a crowbar or place its hands around the reader's throat, constricting their larynx and squeezing the air and the very life out of them. The page, the ink, will not verbally abuse and belittle the reader, crushing their soul over a period of several years. In life, there is no closing the cover when one has had enough for one session, there is no returning life to the shelf and walking away, leaving it and forgetting about it forever. No, you must find the words to articulate such things with the vivid intensity that will make the reader unable to leave, make them believe, make them feel that they are experiencing it, perhaps to find such powerful expression that the reader will *actually feel* those same things, experience that very acute and specific pain, not through empathy, not through sympathy, but by drawing them to that same place and making them *actually live it*. You have to make them see through your eyes and walk in your shoes.

He needed a break. Needed to clear his head, to regain his focus. Yes, he had a deadline looming, but he'd never make it like this. Just a few minutes of doing something – anything – to take his mind off the task at hand would provide the vital distraction, vital space, that would enable him to return to his undertaking refreshed and reinvigorated. All he needed was a few minutes' distance between himself and this piece of work.

He rose from his chair, rubbing his eyes again. He needed rest. But there was work to be done. He headed over to the coffee machine in the corner of the office and hit the buttons that would yield up the strongest, sweetest brew available.

Returning to his desk, Tim pondered how best to amuse himself and to take his mind off work. Opening a new browser on his desktop, he went to the BBC Sports pages and scanned the F1 headlines. He wasn't nearly the petrolhead he used to be, and didn't even watch all of the Grand Prix races any more, let alone get up at ridiculous times to watch them live on the box, but he still liked to keep up with what was happening. He soon grew bored flicking through the sports pages but had no wish to return to writing his report just yet. His coffee was still too hot to drink. This awful muck definitely had an optimum temperature, which was below the throat-scorching heat at which it was ejected by the machine, but well above the tepid point it usually dropped to all

would provide the vital distraction, vital space, that would enable him to return to his undertaking refreshed and reinvigorated. All he needed was a few minutes' distance between himself and this piece of work.

He rose from his chair, rubbing his eyes. He headed into the kitchen and fired up the kettle while scooping coffee into his three-cup caffetierre and taking the bag of sugar from the cupboard: he was going to make the strongest, sweetest brew possible.

Returning to his desk, Anthony threw a CD into the disc drive. He had found it increasingly difficult to write while listening to music in recent years and considered it a shame that his two main passions in life, reading and music, both appeared to conflict with his occupation. Not that he could really complain: he much preferred working from home and being able to work in his own environment, in his dressing gown and slippers if he so chose, to being stuck in some shitty office. He sat back and let the strains of Girls Against Boys' sleazecore classic *Cruise Yourself* slither around his being. Opening a new browser on his desktop, he went to the BBC News pages: he liked to keep up with current affairs, and often found inspiration for his own writing within the stories.

too quickly.

Moving from the sports section, Tim cast his eye over a few news stories. He didn't really have much of an interest in current affairs; the news was depressing and politics was shit. But he needed to pass the time and bad news might make him feel better about himself, he reasoned. Should he feel guilty for revelling in others' misfortunes?

Police have launched a murder investigation after the discovery of a teenager's body at a house in Leeds.

Officers were called to the property on Compton Row in the Harehills area of the city at 1545 BST on Monday where they found the teenage girl dead.

Investigations are continuing at the scene and neighbours reported hearing a disturbance before police arrived.

It was all too depressing, and only reaffirmed his prejudices. Death and despair everywhere, fundamentalists bombing the fuck out of one another – and innocent civilians – for no obvious good reason; children and teenagers and old ladies being mugged, raped and murdered in every city, town and village every night; the government

Real-life: that's what people identify with, he thought, and working to this adage, he tried to pepper his work with as much harsh reality as he feasibly could. It had been a formula that had worked for him so far, and he liked the way crossing his fictional writing with his reviews and the like served to build some kind of cross-genre intertextuality.

Sock it to me lifestyle...

Police have launched a murder investigation after the discovery of a teenager's body at a house in Leeds.

Officers were called to the property on Compton Row in the Harehills area of the city at 1545 BST on Monday where they found the teenage girl dead.

Investigations are continuing at the scene and neighbours reported hearing a disturbance before police arrived.

I know what happens now...
Slurping down the last of his strong, hot coffee and deciding he had been a fool to tell his publisher that he had a complete manuscript available when all he had was the first three chapters and a handful of notes – not even a solid plot, Anthony decided that what he really needed to do at this juncture

trying to find new ways of screwing honest, hard-working individuals like himself out of their hard-earned cash by means of new stealth taxes – some not so stealthy, too – while making even bigger handouts to state spongers who were living off *his* wages, damn it; doom-mongers and green liberals all jumping on the global warming bandwagon and spreading panic... Tim didn't like to consider such things. Life was short and life was bleak, he knew this and didn't need reminding, and certainly didn't need scaremongers trying to tell him how to live his life, to stop driving, to turn his heating down or off. If it was cold, he would be warm. Man had evolved to master his environment. It wasn't that he was in complete denial over the global warming issue, he just didn't like to be told what to do. Besides, there was little he as an individual could do. It was down to the large companies and the industrial manufacturers in the developing world to act, and for governments to legislate if they wanted to see real change. Perhaps they would in time, but for now, he was buggered if he was doing to sift through his rubbish to recycle stuff, and besides, it wasn't going to have a significant effect on him. Maybe the next

was to capture the tedium of everyday life. This was something so many people could relate to. It couldn't fail. Yes, Michel Houellebecq had done a brilliant job of doing something similar in *Whatever*, as had Michael Bracewell in *Perfect Tense*, but Anthony considered his style to be radically different from either of theirs, and thus his target audience was different. Besides, there had been something of a trend for 'office' novels during the late 1990s and continuing into the new millennium, as Matt Thorne's *8 Minutes Idle*, Matt Beaumont's *e* and Douglas Coupland's *Microserfs* evidence, and these represented just a small handful of examples.

But he needed an angle. He didn't need to create a character so obnoxious that readers would turn off – even if the obnoxious aspect was done to good effect like the lead character in Irvine Welsh's *Filth* – but he did need to make his character work for him, to provide a vehicle for something.

As the CD spun out its final track, it came to him. Yes it was simple. Oh, but it would be effective.

After an hour's typing, he took another break. He was thirsty. It was time for a cup of tea.

generation, or the generation after that, but not now.

The Foo Fighters' track 'The Best of You' rattled from his pocket for the umpteenth time that day. He loved that song – it rocked – but he was beginning to tire of its polyphonic yet stunted ring-tone version intruding into his life every five minutes. He checked the name on the incoming call. It was Amy, his 'better half.' They had been together almost eight years now – long enough for him to have known almost instinctively that it would have been her ringing this time.

"Hi, Ames," he said, half sighing, half croaking, his voice cracked with fatigue.

"Hey," she chirruped back.

"Hey," he echoed back, as he commonly did. It bought time, breathing space, signalled to her that he was listening, like a call-and-response of 'Copy,' 'Roger.'

"I was just wondering what time you'd be home for tea tonight," she said in her usual even, gentle tone.

He sighed and rubbed his tired, itchy eyes again. Amy liked her routine. Daily, she called around 3.30 or 4pm to enquire when he'd be home, although he was rarely able to give a specific answer. There was the small matter of work to be done, followed by

Sipping his Earl Grey he turned on the television. Flicking through the Freeview channels, he came to The Hits. It was some kind of 'alternative hour,' and the Foo Fighters were on. Anthony hated the Foo Fighters. The first album had been throwaway lightweight guitar pop and inoffensive enough, but hadn't really done much to turn his head around. It certainly hadn't suggested world domination a decade hence. What was it that riled him so? After a moment's contemplation, it came to him: Grohl had sold out. Nirvana had not only been a one-band musical revolution in cultural terms, but they hadn't compromised, musically or in any other sense. Post-Nirvana, Grohl had transmogrified into the acceptable face of corporate rock: acceptable to the kids, because the Foo Fighters made rock music; acceptable to the suits and the mainstreamers because they rocked but not too much, and besides, that Dave Grohl, he's such a *nice guy*.

Disgusted, annoyed and feeling his blood pressure rise, Anthony flicked through a few more channels. Yup, 57 channels and nothin' on. In fact, at last count, he had noted over a hundred channels. And still fucking nothing on. All the quantity and no quality.

the invariably hellish commute home, which could take anything from forty minutes to an hour and a half.

"I dunno," he replied after a pause. "I've got a lot on at the moment."

"Ok, do you think you'll be home before eight-ahuh?" she asked, her voice rising at the end and a small not-quite-laugh following the last syllable. He pictured her, smiling as she did, her nose wrinkled a little and her eyes half-closed, an endearing expression which he had been fond of from the outset when they had met some seven years ago. How time flew! He had been in his early twenties then, and having recently relocated following the securing of a decent job in Manchester, Tim had been on the brink of embarkation on his career proper.

"I don't know," he reiterated. "I hope so, but I wouldn't like to say for definite."

"Ok, well I thought we might have chops tonight and they grill in no time, so I shall wait until you get in before starting the tea."

"Fine."

"Call me when you're leaving work?"

"Sure."

"Ok, I'll speak to you later,

Turning to BBC News 24, as he frequently did in times of boredom or exasperation, Anthony decided to check the headlines again and see what new developments there had been, what was going on in the world.

Gordon Brown has been accused of "cynical pre-election politics" over his visit to British forces in Iraq.

Shadow defence secretary Liam Fox said Mr Brown preferred a photo opportunity in Basra to keeping his promise to tell MPs first about planned troop cuts.

He said the PM used the armed forces as a "political football." Sir John Major also questioned the timing of the announcement and Mr Brown's visit.

But No 10 said it was "preposterous" to suggest the PM was playing politics. The prime minister's official spokesman said he had always planned to go to Iraq as part "of the normal process of government."

During his visit, Mr Brown said that UK forces in Iraq were to be cut by 1,000 by 2008.

The Ministry of Defence has since

bye."

"Yeah, bye."

He couldn't help it, he knew he sounded 'off.' The simple fact was that he had been feeling decidedly fractious lately, and it was difficult to pinpoint the exact reasons why. And because he didn't know, he felt he couldn't really talk about it with Amy – what was there to say? It was his problem, and he didn't want to push it onto her. She had her own things going on, namely the fact that she hadn't worked in over three months now. It wasn't that she was unemployable or lacked skills: she had been in a number of office jobs between her degree and her belated MA, but following her second graduation, she had simply drifted through temp jobs and short fixed-terms contracts. It was difficult for Tim not to show any resentment toward her, given that he was carrying her financially, and she didn't even spend her time on the house – or herself – while he was at work, and job hunting didn't seem to have appeared on her agenda in some time now.

He turned back to the screen once more.

"Sod it," he muttered to himself.

He picked up his coat from the back of his chair and made his excuse

confirmed that figure includes the 500 troops whose withdrawal was announced in July - 270 of whom are already home.

The remaining 230 and a further 500 should be home for Christmas, Mr Brown said. After that, 4,500 UK troops will remain, at the Basra Airport base.

Anthony's attention was cut through by the sounds of the telephone.

"Hello?"

"Alright?" It was Simon.

They went back a good few years, back to their university days. They had enjoyed some good times together, mostly centred around the local pubs and student bars, staying up late, hopelessly drunk and ranting indefatigably about obscure music and cult fiction. On meeting in the first year, it had rapidly become apparent that Simon and Anthony shared quite similar tastes in both. They had spent many afternoon and evenings in one another's halls and houses, listening to the most underground sounds they could find for one another, their audio experiences occasionally enhanced with a joint or two.

Simon hadn't wanted to return to his hometown of Newark,

to Andy Price as he passed him in the doorway into the main office – "yeah, just going to pick up some files... won't be back in this afternoon now."

"Alright, mate, see yer," Andy cheered.

Tim was free. He was going home.

He slowed his pace as he passed through the main office, allowing himself to do something he rarely – never – did: to cast his eye over the others who worked there, some of whom he knew by sight but not by name, many of whom he had never seen in his life. It struck him as strange that he should spend so many hours in this building with all these people, and yet only know a handful of them to speak to.

Heading toward the exit, he spied some quality totty, but his favourite remained the busty tart on reception who did a great line in short skirts and low-cut tops. How he wanted to bury his face in those tits of hers! He never would, of course: he was with Amy and one hundred percent committed and faithful. But she was dependable, reserved, austere even, and Sindy seemed to him to represent everything Amy wasn't.

He'd not swap Amy for the world, but things had been growing a

embarrassed by the small shithole market town, the name of which was an anagram of 'wanker,' and like Anthony, had remained in Sheffield on graduation. And so, despite Simon's having gone 'straight' and selling out to The Man, they had remained friends, and although they saw one another considerably less frequently these days, still enjoyed lengthy alcohol-fuelled discussions about music, books and this and that, this and that, this and that.

"Hey, how's it going?" asked Anthony.

"Good," replied Simon.

"Cool."

Neither had ever been particularly adept and communication by telephone.

"Fancy a pint?"

"Sure." Anthony knew he had work to do, but a pint or three would probably help loosen him up. He often wrote better with a few drinks in him. "Where, when?"

"Frog and Parrot in an hour?"

Anthony checked his watch. It was ten past four. "Done."

"See you there."

Ant put the phone down. Sensibly, he should eat something before heading out. But he wasn't feeling sensible. He was too busy

little stale of late: maybe to swap for just one night... No, no, it was wrong. He pushed these thoughts from his mind. He gave Sin a nod as he passed and she returned with a saucy wink and he was boning up in his suit trousers.

What is it about that girl? He mused as he traversed the concourse toward his sporty convertible BMW. He wasn't sure, but he'd like to take her for a ride! His thoughts were pure filth as looked at the shiny vehicle that was his pride and joy.

Reminding himself that he was a good boy and pulling his jacket across to disguise his embarrassing bulge, he figured he'd have to release his muck back home – preferably with Amy's assistance, but more likely, as had been more often the case recently, with thoughts of Sindy and a box of Tesco mansize facial tissues.

***

On his way home, he had called into a petrol station and purchased a bunch of flowers in the hope that this would help him woo his long-term girlfriend. The hour long drive in top to tail commuter traffic surrounded by tossers in more expensive suits driving better, faster, more expensive cars than his had raised his ire, but had failed to

wrestling with his literary dilemmas to contemplate food. All he really wanted was beer and a good rant. Things usually fell together after – or during – a beer and a rant.

An eternal student at heart, Anthony had remained near the Broomhill area, so it was a manageable walk, if done briskly, to the Frog and Parrot on Division Street in the Devonshire Quarter of the city. It wasn't the best pub in the world by any stretch, but being a Greene King pub, it wasn't too self-consciously fashionable and at least did a reasonable line in real ales. He considered this to be particularly important.

Not liking to smoke in the house, and being forbidden by law to smoke in the pub, he lit a cigarette and started on his way. The beer was calling.

***

A wall of photographs and albums in frames signed by local artists – Human League, Jarvis Cocker, Def Leppard – occupied one side of the bar, while the remainder of the wall space was plastered with posters and flyers for events, club nights and gigs: Kid Arney and the Harley; Walker, a 'bass-heavy 3-piece rocking you the

abate his burning lust. The fact of the matter was, he was a seething mass of hormones and he just wanted his hole, but his conscience wouldn't let him take it just anywhere, even if he had possessed the capacity to pull just like that, which he very much doubted he did. And he was fucked if he was going to pay for it!

Bursting in through the front door, he was more than a little disappointed to find Amy in her worn towelling dressing gown and nightie. Her hair was unbrushed and she didn't look like she'd been up very long. She didn't look exactly over the moon to see him either, her expression a feint mix of surprise and boredom.

"I wasn't expecting you home so early," she drabbed.

At that moment it dawned on Tim that he'd not called her to forewarn her of his departure from work, as had been promised – quite forgetting that his early finish had been because he'd wanted to surprise her.

"I brought you these," he said feebly, drawing the flowers, price tag still attached, from behind his back.

"Thanks," she said with a weak, wan, forced smile.

His horn withered rapidly. It wasn't just the manky, faded-to-grey nightie or her lack of makeup. It

mostest'; Pifco, promising '2-piece Fall-like magic in lab coats...' The Beatles' 'Yesterday' drifted tiredly from the jukebox.

"I fucking hate my job," spat Simon by way of an opening gambit.

Anthony was sympathetic – to a point. After all, he had *chosen* to go and work for some faceless multinational financial institution.

"I hate absolutely fucking everything about it," Simon continued without drawing breath, somehow managing to inhale a third of his pint *as if by osmosis* as he spoke. "I hate the work, I hate the culture, I hate the fucking people I work with, my boss is a complete cunt, I hate the office itself, I even hate having to walk halfway down fucking Eccleshall Road to get there every fucking morning! I'm so tempted to just quit and get a job elsewhere."

He said he was ambitious... so he accepts the process...

"I hate to say it," said Anthony in a measured tone, "but I have a hunch most jobs – most conventional office-based jobs, the sort you do, and the sort you're thinking about – are all more or less equally bad. You could quit and get another job doing admin for another company, but the chances are it'll be a case of 'same shit,

wasn't simply the mugs, half-full of day-old tea, bowls lined with cereal dried and encrusted onto the ceramic sides and crumb-covered plates at strategic points around the living room and kitchen – and no doubt the rest of the house. He could overlook all that when driven by his dick. No, it was Amy's indifference that was like a slap in the face.

"Just off up to get changed," he said flatly.

The bed was unmade. Amy's pyjama trousers lay straddled across the corner of the bed, her pyjama top on the floor. Tim was particularly keen on that pyjama top, as it was made of relatively fine fabric, and, being powder-blue in hue, meant that her nipples were visible through it, at least in the right light. Despite their lack of recent activity in the bedroom, Tim had fantasised about Amy in these particular pyjamas, scenarios in which he had thrown the curtains open and pressed her against the window as he took her from behind, her breasts cold as they pressed against the glass... or situations whereby she had taken a shower in that powder-blue cotton top which had become transparent under the spray and he had secretly photographed her as she had touched herself, then stripped and soaped

different office,' and that you'll be as pissed off with the next job and the next lot of people you work with just the same after three, six months or whatever."

Simon sluiced down half of his remaining pint in a single gulp and looked thoughtful for a moment.

"Yeah, but are you saying you're loving your work?"

"Yeah, I suppose I am," Ant said, a grin spreading.

"But you're always skint," countered his friend. "You can't enjoy being broke."

"True," Barker conceded, "but at least I can say I've not sold out."

"Pah!" Simon snorted derisively. "I've not sold out, I just accept that I need money to live, and the way to obtain that money is by working."

"...in a job you hate," concluded Anthony. "In short, you've accepted the process and thus become part of the machine. Ergo, you've sold out."

"Yes, I've accepted the process," Smith agreed, "but I've not sold out. I'm just aware of the fact that there's no alternative."

"There's always an alternative," Ant proffered.

"Yeah, yeah," jeered Si. "I

herself down… other images he forced himself to deny… sleepsploitation and somnophilia, BDSM and worse besides… *You don't have to say please…* His long years between girlfriends had driven him to explore the world of internet pornography, and while those years were now but a dim and distant memory, so far off they felt to him as though they were part of another life, even scenes he had seen in a film, perhaps, their effects had burned deeper into his psyche than he had ever realised or would ever, ever admit…

That evening, they ate in near silence, with only the occasional 'pass the salt' punctuating the clatter of cutlery against crockery.

Amy seemed absorbed in her own thoughts and Tim didn't want to – didn't know how to – break through the walls she was constructing as partitions within their domicile. Communication had never really been his forte. He wanted to forget that. It pained him to think about his past, the awkward kid who never had a girlfriend, spent his youth, and his teenage years – and his early twenties – tied to his mother's apron strings. He winced with embarrassment at the mention, or the idea of his old self.

mean the fact remains that no one gives a shit about their work, everybody hates their job, *I* hate my job, you hated yours so much you quit and became a pauper… 'nother pint?"

"Thought you'd never ask."

Returning presently with two pints of Frog's Bollocks, Simon noticed Tony was looking distant. He commented as much.

"Hmm, would you say it's possible for an experimental work to have emotional depth? Or, moreover, is it appropriate for such a text to carry emotional depth - should the content more compatibly match the style?"

"Why would that be incompatible?"

"I'm not sure… I suppose for some reason I associate 'experimental' with fiction that's as much *about* challenging the establishment, etc., or revolution, in terms of content as well as form."

"*Mother Night* was hugely experimental and was still highly emotional…"

Embarrassed by his ignorance, Anthony ventured to ask, "Who wrote that?"

"Brecht," said Simon with a hint of smugness before correcting himself: "Wait, I don't mean *Mother*

But he had put all of that behind him; he had a career, and in Amy, who was slim and blonde and quiet, he had a partner he could be proud of when he was out, especially with the boys. Recent years, during which he had made these developments and acquisitions that marked him as a success and were a fuck-you to all those who had mocked or, worse still, ignored him in school. He didn't want to go back there, but was at a loss in the here and now. He hated rows and didn't want anything to ripple the millpond of his easy domestic life.

When had things got so difficult? Why was life so hard? Tim reflected that things had been so much more straightforward for him as a child. Responsibility was a grind.

They watched television till gone eleven and went to bed without shagging.

***

The following morning, Tim was still sore from the previous night's rejection, and his balls ached chronically. Once again, he was finding it hard to focus on his work, and something in his innards wasn't quite right. He struggled on for a while

Night. I mean *Mother Courage*. *Mother Night* is a Vonnegut book."

They rattled on in this fashion, veering between dismantling capitalism and exploding popular urban myths through discourse on literature and the latest Shellac album (– not bad, claimed Si – not a patch on *1000 Hurts*, Ant counterclaimed) for another five pints before Simon suddenly saw it was almost a quarter to eleven.

"Gotta go, man," he said. "I've got to be at work in good time Tomorrow."

"Pussy," jibed Ant.

"Oh, sod off!" laughed Simon. "You have no idea..."

"Superpussy! Superpussy! Superpussy!"

Barker downed his dregs and left with his friend. He had work to do – not tomorrow, but now.

***

Does the body rule the mind or does the mind rule the body? Does the writer create and own the character or does the character take temporary control of the author? Or is the character's identity forged in the mind of the reader?

before conceding finally that it was no good.

He went into the gents: for the first time in a fortnight he was busting for a crap. Pushing past some cret who was leaning against the hand dryer to type a text message while listening to his MP3 player at outrageous volume, he came to the first cubicle and was dismayed to find the bog blocked, the water had risen to within an inch of the rim and was abrim with shredded paper and rancid stinking partially-dissolved pieces of shit.

The second cubicle was without toilet paper, but the third and final trap was ok – a few dried bogies smeared and encrusted onto the chipboard laminate divider walls, but nothing serious and thus eminently usable. Parking his arse on the clammy plastic seat, he could still hear the bozo's lamearsed indie music bleeding from his earphones. The kid would be deaf before he hit 40 through listening to music at that volume for prolonged periods, thought Tim. And the profusion of half-arsed limp-wristed guitar music was really beginning to bug him. While he had a soft spot for some of the leaders in the field, like Razorlight and Hard-Fi, and even quite liked the odd stand-out tune by a few others, the market had reached a point

The fact is that there are no facts. Given that any factual account or document is subject to a lengthy sequence of filters, both on the part of the creator and the receiver, how reliable can any account be considered? The camera never lies... but the image itself can be subject to manipulation. We know this much to be true.

So who precisely is narrating this, who's painting the picture? And whose account do you believe? In fiction, for it to work, there has to be an element of truth to lend a text credibility. But when there are no facts, what is truth?

The dilemmas of the 'creative' process swam around in Anthony's mind when he surfaced groggily, checking the bedside clock. 7:13. Still early. He had a tendency to wake quite early, no matter how late he had gone to bed and no matter how much alcohol he had consumed the night he had consumed the night before, and this morning was no different. Despite having stayed up typing and drinking and dredging ever deeper into the more unlistenable corners of his music collection as the night wore on, finally retiring at 3:30 and half a bottle of gin down, he was pleased to awake feeling only mildly shit.

of saturation, and the increase in quantity seemed to reflect an inverse turn of quality. Indie was the new rap or the new dance, or whatever.

He took a dump and felt his sphincter pucker under the exertion of depositing such a dry, prickly turd, the first shit he'd had for almost a week. The single black pellet splashed in the water. Perhaps his doctor had been right; perhaps he was stressed, perhaps he did need to eat more fibre, and to drink more water. But he felt awkward eating at work, especially the kind of health food that his colleagues would gyp him about. He didn't like to draw attention to himself, and being seen tucking into a McDonald's every once in a while was a lot butcher than shuffling rabbit food round a Tupperware box. Image matters.

Similarly, taking on fluids made him need to pass water. He didn't have time for things like that in his busy schedule, with long hours of driving, and public lavatories – including those in the office – repulsed him. Plus, making trips to the toilet could be seen as weakness, and besides, getting one's tadger out in the company of other men was wrong... but then, locking oneself in a cubicle to pee also looks a bit weird. Such a minefield! Better to cut if from the

He creaked downstairs, made himself a caffetierre of strong Javan and shuffled up to the office, wearily rubbing his eyes. His skin felt rough and dry, his eyes sensitive and watery. He was exhausted, and this was reflected in his sallow appearance reflected in the monitor as he fired up the PC.

Sipping the steaming coffee, he reviewed his work from the previous night. Some of it, he felt was rather good. Although long nights and alcohol did little for his typing skills, they did often enable him to write without the inhibitions that had a habit of stifling and stilting his output when he was in a more normal, that is to say, sober and entirely wakeful, frame of mind. Nighttime had a way of placing him in an altogether different place, one in which he got wired and typed like a maniac, his mechanism of self-censorship bypassed as his creativity and his hands were hardwired together to turn him into a writing machine.

Of course, there would always be editing required, revisions to me made after one of his frenzied typefests, but that was all an integral part of the process; switch off, splurge, tweak and hopefully hey presto. He didn't like to edit too hard as he felt that if overworked the immediacy of

equation where possible. Image matters.

Tim didn't stop to consider where this all came from; he knew his parents were old-fashioned, rather uptight, his mother even downright neurotic, it didn't do to dwell on these matters. No good could come of it. The past was the past, it should remain there. Tim was on the up. His life was good, and he would show the world that he was a success. Yes, he had a decent job, and now he wanted to reap the rewards, to pull up to country pubs in a sleek convertible and step out in some neat duds and turn heads. The men would bristle with envy and the chicks would go moist knowing that the man before them was a success, so fuck you. So what if a flash car was considered by some to be a penis extension? Fuck them and their petty jealousies. He'd earned it. And so what if some considered a smart suit and a nice house 'showing off'? Again, he'd earned it and it was his right to wear his achievements for all to see. Yes, the suit was a status symbol. But he didn't need the past and had erased it from his memory, some intentionally, some he had simply forgotten. Whatever, it didn't matter. It was gone now and he stood shielding his eyes from the sun as he looked to the bright,

the prose would likely be subdued or lost altogether. But he wasn't so averse to editing for overall smoothness of flow, for sense and readability, he wasn't convinced by Kerouac's opinion of 'first thought best thought,' especially in light of the fact that Kerouac had written an awful lot of overly-long, self-indulgent meandering cack.

He scratched his head and rose from his seat. He needed some music, if only to cover the silence. But music was more than a mere space-filler. Ant found music had the capacity to be transcendental, and wherever he was and in whatever frame of mind, the right song or soundscape could take him to another place completely, not simply a distraction from the humdrum of his surroundings, but out of his mindset, out of his own skin and into another world beyond the physical realm.

Selecting *Love* by Foetus, he let the incongruous blend of harpsichord and grating industrial guitars tease his senses while he considered his next move. Where did he want to take this piece? Yes, he wanted to capture the ennui of the corporate grind, but he wanted to go beyond that... he wanted to also reveal the contradictions inherent within people and expound his

bright future. But he simply couldn't concentrate.

He decided to take his lunch early, and throwing *The Back Room* by Editors into the car stereo, went for a spin to clear his head.

***

It was just another day at the office. Tim sat and stared vacantly at his monitor. He felt tired and grotty. The report simply wasn't happening. He tried in vain to stifle a yawn, then rubbed his eyes with his thumb and forefinger. His skin felt rough and dry, his eyes sensitive and watery. He was exhausted, and this was reflected in his sallow appearance. The text was beginning to drift before his eyes as he read it again and again. The text was beginning to drift before his eyes as he read it again and again.

He needed something to pick him up, but caffeine brought on migraines, and besides, he hated the taste of both tea and coffee – not that the dishwater that the machine down the office spat out into little plastic cups resembled any tea or coffee he had ever tasted or smelled. Although he never drank it himself, the aroma that drifted from his colleagues' desks turned his stomach, made him want to

belief that the more normal a person appears, the more fucked up they are on the inside. The beautiful people aren't so beautiful when you scratch the surface...

Cunts, one and all.

***

I wanted to create a text that contained everything. I didn't want to just give a snapshot of modern society, but to condense the whole of that society into a single book. And I wasn't going to be satisfied with just describing the sensations, the alienation, the confusion, I wanted to recreate it with an intensity that drags on the nerves and screams at the senses. I wanted to produce a work that instils in the reader a sense of overkill, oversaturation, to induce a dizziness and bewilderment. Waking up and being bombarded with news before getting in a car and driving to work where you open your emails to find three dozen spam mails all advertising viagra is one thing – yes, it's overwhelming. But describing the sensation in narrative is, by and large, quite underwhelming. I wanted to overwhelm. I wanted to create a text that provokes a very definite response, that's both physical and psychological.

hurl. More than a pick-me-up, he needed rest. Perhaps he should work from home and grab a power-nap before resuming work on the report.

Just then, Andy's head appeared above the monitor.

"Alright, mate?" he beamed.

"Not really," Tim sighed.

I wanted to make it too much. I wanted to create a text that had the capacity to inflict pain.

I didn't want to suffer alone. although in the end, we all suffer alone, one way or another. And while the end may yet be a long way off, I am suffering. And alone.

***

***

Tim sat and rubbed his eyes with his thumb and forefinger. His skin felt rough and dry, his eyes sensitive and watery. He was exhausted, and this was reflected in his sallow appearance. He had spent the last week and a half driving long-distance between the sites he was surveying for this report he was working on, and it was really beginning to take its toll on him now.

He had woken up feeling dog rough, the embodiment of every cliché regarding the hangover from hell ever invented.

It was strange: going out and getting thoroughly rat-arsed like that just wasn't his style. Yes, he had been putting away three or four cans on an evening recently in a futile attempt to relax, but the grogginess that had affected him most mornings was ample deterrent from allowing himself to consume more. Besides, Amy

The body of the text was coming along nicely, Ant thought, but he felt as though something still wasn't quite right. He felt as though he had succeeded in conveying the humdrum existence of the average anonymous chairpounder, but had so far done little to suggest that work fucks you up. He wanted to build his character, and then to knock him down, to place him in situations that would force him to crumble, to dissolve in a crisis of confidence and to drown in a miasma of confusion. But how... he tried to put the issue out of mind and focus on other important matters, namely a title.

A good title is important, and a good title that's been a good title for someone else first is always a winning formula. Taking a song title, for instance, is a particularly good strategy, in that it provides a form of referencing. It didn't necessarily matter

disapproved of him getting drunk – not that he was really predisposed to it. Why had he acted so out of character? Through the blinding industrial-force headache, he peered through the fog in an attempt to grab some kind of recollection of the events of the previous night, but nothing came to light. It was a complete blank. As the panic rose within him, so did his bile.

A sweat broke on his brow and with a sudden and violent hiccough, a small patty of pink vomit appeared beside him on the arm of the settee. He hadn't got this wrecked since he'd been in college, and then only once or twice. He'd vowed never again. He hated feeling like this, and the shame and embarrassment that had consumed him when the stories from those blank hours came back... never had he wanted so badly to curl up and die.

The Foo Fighters' track 'The Best of You' blared out once more. While he loved that song – it rocked – he was in no mood for its jarringly trebly ring-tone version fucking his skull right now. He checked the name on the incoming call. It was Amy.

Feeling like he would spew again, he hung up. *Shit*, he thought as the panic gripped him.

Instead he crawled out from under the duvet he had no recollection

whether or not the majority 'got' the reference. A good title is a good title, and besides, stowing subtle references across a text is both fun and subversive, like planning a children's hunt for Easter eggs or laying land-mines in the desert. And why not?

You want to leave it but you can't forget about it... he couldn't leave it alone, He cut and he pasted, he shunted text around from one page to the next, he chopped and changed, deleted and rewrote. It was within his power to change things, to write a fictional history... what else does a writer do but change, edit and manipulate the words at his disposal?

A dilemma faced Tony, and it was proving to be a major stumbling block in the development of his narrative. He wanted so desperately to capture and convey the tedium, the ennui of the humdrum existence of the chairpounding prole. But how to render tedium in a way that's interesting to the reader? He wasn't entirely sure if it was possible. Or, if it was, if it was possible given his limitations as an author who was still learning his craft. But what writer isn't? No author is ever complete. And such is the nature of influence.

In a transmuted re-enactment of the Oedipal cycle, the author

25

of taking from the spare room – why had he slept on the sofa instead of in there? – and stumbled to the bathroom. He pissed long as hard, but his guts were churning like crazy and he couldn't tell if he was going to spew or shit or both together. He sat on the bog with the household bucket on his lap as he gushed forth from every orifice. Where was Amy? What time was it anyway?

Having emptied himself for certain, passing water out of his anus and his chops, Tim wiped himself down, then weakly got up and went in search of his girlfriend. Just as he spied a note on the kitchen table, his mobile rang. It was work. His manager wasn't happy. It was almost ten and where the fuck was he? He needed that report by 2pm.

"Yeah, just got caught up with a few things... yeah, working from home. I'll be in before lunch, and yeah, I'll be sure you get the report."

He rubbed his eyes with his thumb and forefinger. His skin felt rough and dry, his eyes sensitive and watery. His phone rang again. It was Amy.

"Hey..." he croaked.

She gave him short shrift. This was unusual. She was meek by nature, and when displeased was more

necessarily perceives the work of his esteemed precursors as incomplete and through a process of completion, diminishment, rejection and reclamation, devours and assimilates the precursor, pillaging and ultimately obliterating their work before ultimately claiming the forefather's position. Tony's biggest obstacle to his creativity was his own knowledge of that which had gone before and his awareness, however incomplete, of the theories of influence. The weight of the canon bearing down on him had, at times, a truly stultifying effect on his capacity to produce. He didn't believe in inspiration, but often struggled to function simply as a writing machine.

Ant was a frustrated man. The mass media said nothing to him about his life, yet was emblematic of western culture as a whole, spewing out endless garbage, sonic and visual landfill, a predigested slurry of fast food for the mind, and the narcotized masses lapped it up. Flicking through the racks in his local HMV, he had struggled to find much of interest while being jostled by collegegoers and new suits who'd graduated from college to take their positions as lifelong chairpounders. As they milled about mindlessly, preening and comparing the memory on their i-Pods, they

commonly given to dispensing the silent treatment than actually expressing her dissatisfaction verbally. Anger wasn't really in her emotional vocabulary. But right here, right now, Tim was taken aback by her tone which was bordering on the overtly hostile.

"Where the hell were you?"

Confused, flustered and feeling like death, Tim didn't know what to say: he wasn't even sure exactly what she was asking.

"Er, when?"

"Last night!" Amy was borderline hysterical, her voice shaking to the extent that it barely sounded like her on the phone. "You didn't come home, you never phoned, you didn't answer your phone, I rang the office and Andy said you'd gone home early, no-one knew where you were...."

"Shit," he groaned, "I just don't know."

"What do you mean, you don't know?"

"I mean I really can't remember. I left work... and the next thing I know I woke up on the sofa."

"But I don't understand..." Amy was practically sobbing now.

"I don't either," Tim levelled with a grimace.

"So who were you with?" she

would occasionally pick up a DVD or a game, the only physical media they sunk any money into and bawl at one another that they liked the song that was blaring from the in-house speakers playing the week's playlist of mass-marketed 'Indie.' Yeah, celebrate the mediocrity... Worst of all was the local scene – any local scene, every one a facsimile of every other local scene full of spotty teens emulating the spotty teens they received friend requests from on MySpace as they made their meteoric ascent to chart stardom for One Night Only... It wasn't just music, it was art it was literature it was food it was culture: life had lost its flavour. And so he desired to simultaneously reflect the turgid workaday repetition of the everyday realities against a backdrop of magnolia, while injecting some dynamism into the stagnating form that 'the novel' had become.

Really, what was the future of literature? Was there even a future for literature? The Internet had been hailed as the future of everything, the way forward. Yes, and factory smog is a sign of progress. But progress always comes at a price. Global communications were supposed to make life easier, faster, without boundaries... but the actuality had

persisted.

"I really don't know... I don't remember anything," Tim squawked, his agitation rising.

"I waited and waited before having tea," she sniffled. "I was so worried... I thought... I didn't know what to think..."

"I, look, I have to go," he cut her short. "Got to get to work. I've seriously fucked up."

"What...?" she gasped. Amy was unaccustomed to Tim using such strong language in this type of context, but there was something else that perturbed her far more deeply. It was his tone... no, something less definable still. He didn't simply sound strained, on edge. He sounded... *different*. Didn't sound like the Tim she knew. His voice sounded hollow, brittle.

"Look, really, I'll sort it and it'll be fine. I'll explain later but really, I have to go," he rattled through clenched teeth, a sweat breaking on his brow. "Call you later, bye."

He killed the call without waiting to hear her reply. He didn't need it. He thought he was going to puke again, but had nothing but dry heaving left in his wracked, desiccated body. So, about last night... he dredged his memories, trying to remember what

proven to be very different. Yes, it was an information superhighway, but the traffic was driving in all directions, a vehicular Brownian motion to extend the metaphor. The postmodern condition became the norm as the truth became buried in an avalanche of conjecture and opinion. And getting oneself heard above all of the background noise, the inane chatter and the insidious propaganda, was nigh on impossible. The world did get smaller, not only in terms of immediacy of contact and the speed with which information could circulate the globe, but in terms of a narrowing of consumer choice. Punch-drunk from the sensory overload that life had become, they had stopped being able to think for themselves, and so bought whatever got shoved down their throats. The corporations with the biggest budgets had the greatest capacity to shove *their* product at the consumer, and so it came to pass that mainstream mediocrity was once again dominating global entertainment.

e-texts were also supposed to be the future. But people still wanted books. Unfortunately, market forces meant that the only books that received significant exposure, and therefore sold in any quantity, was mainstream bilge, he'd just as soon forget. Replay... Over and over and over and over... erase and rewind... Over and over and over and over... but he was drawing blanks. Over and over and over and over...

Confused, flustered and feeling like death, Tim gathered together the papers in the spare room – which, bereft of a bed and containing only his desk, chair, PC and a battered metal filing cabinet he had inherited after an office refit, wasn't so much of a spare room as a makeshift home office – and bundled himself into his car. He hoped the papers included everything he needed for the report he had to submit. He belted up, threw the ignition and put pedal to the metal.

***

While Tim often preferred to dress more casually when he was spending a day on site – a fleece, sturdy boots and Rohan trousers were much more practical when braving the elements, scaling fire escapes and standing on rooftops – his was very much a suit job the rest of the time. Image was important. Looking businesslike is integral to being businesslike: even when he didn't have clients to meet, it was generally considered within the company that

mental chewing gum for consumption on planes and on the beach. And so while the fragmentation of culture that had been said to typify postmodern culture had undoubtedly occurred, the predominant outcome of late capitalism had been a homogenisation of, well, everything.

Exasperated, Anthony decided that there was only one thing for it: to rip it up and start again. Delete! Delete! Yes it was all well and good to convey tedium and normality, but having established that as a backdrop to his 'story,' he was going to have to fuck shit up, to mess with his character, to screw about not only with his creation, but also the chronology.

***

General advice on how to write suggests hitting the reader from the outset with some drama, while also setting the scene and introducing the reader to the central character, but without necessarily divulging too much background information unless it's truly imperative to the subsequent development of both the plot and the character. After all, wading through twenty pages of a person's life story before actually getting to the meat is potentially yawn-inducing, and while it

conventional office attire was the most appropriate mode of dress. He didn't mind this too much. In fact, Tim quite liked the feel of the suit. It made him feel businesslike, professional, capable. It transformed him, like a suit of armour possessed of special powers. He went from being a nobody to being a businessman, a successful man, a commanding, powerful man, the man he wanted to be.

He had no surveying to do today: he had a number of reports to write up, more phone calls to make than he cared to contemplate, and, worst of all, a meeting in the boardroom with the company executives up from London, along with a number of representatives from other regional offices which was scheduled to run from 9am through to midday. It was a chunk he could ill afford to take out of his busy working day.

He wanted to impress: he needed to feel confident, and so had put on his current favourite suit. It was navy, with a really sharp cut.

He arrived a little later than hoped, having been stuck in traffic, and although the meeting had not commenced, most of the other attendees were already present when he got there. He felt a strange sense of déjà vu as he entered the boardroom.

doesn't do to insult the reader's intelligence by assuming they possess the attention span of a goldfish, contemporary readers, who are often short on time and are accustomed to the instant impact of other media, ranging from television and the Internet, as well as snappy short form fiction - flash, even blogs - it's generally unreasonable to expect that they'll persevere beyond the first five pages if they're completely dull.

But such torpor was a vital part of Barker's strategy in this instance. Anthony wanted to reflect the tedium of everyday life, the repetition of the worker's existence, the turgid humdrum routine of the contemporary everyman.

His premise was simple: using a basic method of cut-and-paste combined with careful editing, thus using a framework based around scenic and dialogical repetition, he devised a narrative structure that would endlessly loop back on itself, telling and retelling the same events from slightly different perspectives, with minor alterations each time. The purpose behind this was multifarious. First and foremost, he wanted to problematise the notion of the fixed narrative viewpoint, and instead challenge the reliability of the narrator and 'the author.' He also

A tall, skinny man with short, mousy hair and an ill-fitting suit that hung from his curved meatless shoulders was loitering outside the generously-sized meeting room. The grey suit man greeted Tim, introduced himself as Richard Fiddler, Executive Director, and gesticulated toward a seat midway down the long glass table as they entered. Another man in a charcoal grey suit spoke, and asked Tim if he had met Barry Brown from the Manchester office previously. Tim nodded, as Barry, a chubby ginger bloke with a goatee bounded forward with his hand extended. He displayed an expression like he was meting a friend he hadn't seen in years.

The man in the charcoal suit addresses Tim again, but he doesn't quite catch what he says. He feels a little out of his depth in the company of all of these high-powered executives. To save face, he simply nods again. It's not strictly a compulsion. He simply feels himself nodding as though he was a marionette, his actions controlled by some invisible puppeteer.

Charcoal suit man walks stiffly from the room and returns almost immediately with a small plastic cup full of some foul-smelling brown fluid. It could be the pumped contents of

hoped to problematise the act of reading, and to demand a greater engagement and interaction from the reader. He wanted to get away from the conventions of fiction, specifically genre fiction, from the ubiquitous mediocre crime novel through to the 'questing' blockbusters like *The Da Vinci Code*, in which 'clues' are left strategically throughout the text for the reader to collect and feel smart when they predict the next sequence of events, because life isn't like that. Life isn't formulaic: why should literature be so?

Plot is overrated, he reminded himself as the words flowed from his fingertips.

Moreover, by creating a text that was intentionally mundane and repetitous, Barker believed it would be possible to highlight the endless tedium of the worker's existence, a life based almost solely around routine and a cycle of incentive and reward – but, more insidiously, a mode of living that was little more than an instrument of oppression by which the status quo and the class divides not only remained, but continued to grow ever wider as every man – and woman – strove to better themselves at the expense of someone else. But he wasn't content to simply reflect that nauseating tedium

someone's stomach for all Tim knows, but he instinctively knows it's coffee.

Tim mumbles some incoherent thanks. Charcoal Suit smiles and nods. Charcoal Suit walks around the table and sits down opposite. Tim's feeling hemmed in: Baggy Grey Suit – what was his name again? Fiddler? Dick? Something, whatever – is situated at his left elbow and he feels like he's a piece in a game of chess and the moves available to him are diminishing by the moment.

The meeting commences. It's insufferably dull. There's talk crossing the table, line upon line of factual data and a grasp of figures and certain scientific concepts regarding the deterioration of concrete, the weakening of iron girders, the flammability of certain materials and so on. There are flip charts and flow charts and Microsoft® Office PowerPoint® slideshow presentations.

The presentations were slick. A beefy bloke in a navy pinstripe suit spoke commandingly about the business plan for the forthcoming financial year and the company's 'high-level' strategies.

Some middle-aged bim with goofy teeth and a tasteless trouser-suit is presenting now. She's clearly wise to using Microsoft® Office Fluent™

that the endless routine gives rise to: no, he was bent on creating a text that would replicate that tedium and induce a deep sense of frustration in the reader, who would find themselves reliving the same scenes over and over and over and over.

This isn't Groundhog Day, this is life.

Accusations of producing something boring did concern him, but Baker considered his creation a game of sorts. In the first instance, there would be an abundance of song lyrics and other quotations scattered liberally throughout the text, and while many would be obscure and known only to a certain type of reader – namely one who shared the author's spheres of reference, which were predominantly cult fiction and even culter music, others would be readily identified by those less esoterically informed, drawing from elements of popular culture (although still with a specific emphasis on music). It was his belief that readers would engage in this 'game' and play along, attempting to spot the lifted lines and references, and possibly derive some form of pleasure from this.

"But why?" Simon had asked, when Tony had explained his idea to him over drinks one evening. "I mean,

interface but her presentation is all style and no substance. She goes on for an age, extolling the virtues of 'building relationships,' 'being progressive' and 'proactive cascading.' She's winding down her interim report and the business projections for the next six and 12 months and she's pushing to end with a positive, but instead simply spouts more corporate bromides. The meeting concludes with more rhetorical throat-clearing and back-slapping both metaphorical and literal, faux camaraderie slipping across the smooth surface of the smoked glass table. Tim's glad when he can make his exit: he has reports to write and calls to make.

It's just another day at the office, the same as any other.

***

He needed a break. Needed to clear his head, to regain his focus. Yes, he had a deadline looming, but he'd never make it like this. Just a few minutes of doing something – anything – to take his mind off the task at hand would provide the vital distraction, vital space, that would enable him to return to his undertaking refreshed and reinvigorated. All he needed was a few minutes' distance between himself and

it sounds fun enough and all, but is there really a point to it? What purpose does it serve, ultimately?"

"Is there really a point to anything?" Any had tossed back philosophically.

"Smartarsed cunt," his friend had bantered, but half meant it.

"Ok, but seriously, postmodern fiction is inherently self-referential, and also by its nature draws on the whole gamut of that which went before. High and low art collides and is melded together in an egalitarian melting-pot. Originality is dead, it's passé."

"Yes, but that's arse," Simon had contended.

"I know it's arse, at least to an extent," Ant had countered, "but bear with me."

"If I must." Simon had been particularly testy that night.

"You must," Barker had insisted. "There's a line of thinking that suggests that the only originality possible is through forming new permutations of the old," he explained. "Thus, the merging of seemingly incompatible genres and the referencing of what would appear to be incongruous sources is a form of originality, but it's newness born out of the old."

this piece of work. He had been working on this report for almost three hours now, and he was fagged out after the morning's meeting. Listening back to the recording on his dictaphone was getting him nowhere; his voice was barely audible above the wind, and he had, for some inexplicable reason, been mumbling terribly.

He rubbed his eyes again and returned his bleary pupils to the screen. He had been staring at the screen for what felt like hours. How long it had really been, he was uncertain. The text was beginning to drift before his eyes as he read it again and again.

He rose from his chair, rubbing his eyes again. He needed rest. But there was work to be done. He headed over to the coffee machine in the corner of the office and hit the buttons that would yield up the strongest, sweetest brew available.

What Watson wanted above all was to go home and go to sleep. He felt like he needed a holiday, to get away from it all. Not just from work, but from life. But he knew that this was impossible, simply a pipe dream. There's no getting off the treadmill. And even if there was, what then? It would be necessary to get back on at some point, simply to survive. There were no practical alternatives. There

"All this clever referencing and interweaving of different styles and references is all very well, but what about plot?"

"Plot is overrated," Tone had shot back unhesitatingly.

"You genuinely believe that?" Simon appeared aghast.

"I genuinely believe that," Ant replied evenly. "Can you remember the plot of the books you've read, the films you've seen? The books and films of any kind of quality, that is," he added with a smirk.

Si looked a little nonplussed. "What do you mean?"

"You see, it's often easier to recall the sensations you experienced, how the book or film or whatever made you feel, than to remember what actually happened. And even if you can remember what happened, chances are, you'll misremember the chronology."

"What's your point?"

"Plot's overrated and chronology's vaguely pointless," Barker had boomed bombastically. "But beyond that, most people read or engage with any media as much for escapist purposes as any other," he continued. "And for that reason, style is in many ways more important than content. And content, provided it

was no escaping life. Tim wasn't suicidal. He was simply hacked off and in a rut. And when you're in a rut....

The coffee wasn't doing any good at all. Tim sat and rubbed his eyes with his thumb and forefinger. His skin felt rough and dry, his eyes sensitive and watery. He was exhausted, and this was reflected in his sallow appearance.

6pm rolled around and Tim had had enough. He saved his report onto a USB memory stick which he shoved into his jacket pocket and headed home. He'd work on it from there after tea.

***

It was late morning when Tim arrived at work. It had been a rough night and no mistake. His recollections were a little hazy at best. He had spent the journey attempting to piece together the events of the previous night from a series of flashbacks, none of which was sufficiently substantial for him to really fathom the events that had taken place, let alone their chronology.

He raced through the doors, his perspiration in full spate. *What the fuck was this?* It wasn't that he didn't get nervous – heaven knows he was often

extends beyond plot, is more important than... well, plot. What I'm trying to say is that a text that engages with deeper issues and does something different, makes some kind of social comment or has some kind of emotional impact actually has more resonance, ultimately, than one that's plot-driven. And by text I also mean film, etc., etc., and so on and so forth."

"It's mad. Anthony Barker, *you're* mad." Simon chuckled. "But I suppose it might just work...."

"Oh it will. It won't be easy, but it will: I'm determined it will," Anthony affirmed.

***

It was late morning when Tony surfaced. It had been a rough night and no mistake. His recollections were a little hazy at best. He sat with a coffee attempting to piece together the events of the previous night from a series of flashbacks, none of which was sufficiently substantial for him to really fathom the events that had taken place, let alone their chronology. His head ached.

No man is worth his salt who doesn't labour to make himself obsolete. Ant had clearly laboured hard judging by the potency of his hangover

on edge, hated the tight deadlines, and meetings were and even greater source of stress. But he was conscientious, and never let his work slip, never lost control of himself or a situation. And yet here was, a hungover, nervous wreck, late for work and completely disorganised, belting through the door and up the office with half a ream of loose-leaf papers pinned to his side with his arm, down which rivulets of sweat were running in channels from his armpits.

Arriving at his desk, he dumped the sheaf of print and scribbled notes down on top of keyboard. Collapsing into his chair and firing up the PC, Tim saw Andy's head appeared above the monitor.

"Alright, mate?" he beamed.

"No," Tim slapped.

"No need to bite my head off," Andy said, raising his hands in a gesture of mock surrender. He really could be a twat at times. Much as Tim liked the guy, he had certain issues with him. While he'd never admit it – even to himself – Tim saw Andy as a threat. Yes, Andrew Price was dynamic, go-getting and self-assured, the kind of man Tim aspired to be, pretended to be, tried so desperately to convince himself he was that he even believed it, most of the time....

and the empty bottle of gin on the floor beside the chair at the computer desk.

Firing up the PC, he wondered if he might need to puke, but a few deep, steady breaths seemed to settle him. He was made of sterner stuff – what was just over half a bottle of gin to a man of his constitution? *Had it really only been half a bottle?*

Pouring himself a second coffee from the eight-cup caffetierre he had filled to the brim, he pulled the seat closer to the screen and brought up the document he had been working on from his desktop short cuts. His pirate copy installation of Microsoft® Word was taking longer than usual to load and he feared he'd somehow screwed it up the night before. It wouldn't have been the first time a system crash had corrupted his files, rendered them unopenable. And had he backed up? Had he fuck. He invariably forgot even when sober, so what were the chances of remembering after half a bottle or thereabouts of gin? *Had it really only been half a bottle?*

Eventually the document loaded and he scrolled down past the point he recalled having left off the previous afternoon to review his new additions. Although littered with typographical errors, he was pleasantly surprised to discover than not all of

"Sorry, mate," sighed Tim grimly. "I'm in a spot of bother here," he offered by way of an explanation.

"Yeah?"

"Yeah. Heavy night last night. And now I'm paying for it. And I think I've fucked up. I've got to get this report in by 2pm and I'm struggling. Worse. I'm not even sure if I've got everything."

Price came around and stood with his hands on his hips, stooping slightly so as to resemble a vulture as he hung over Tim's desk.

"What've you got?"

Tim gestured pathetically to the pile on his desk. Andy winced and began to flick through the sheets, fanning them wide and looking studious. The prick.

He was in his prime – or at least, he felt he should have been. So was this really as good as it would get? But Tim was desperate right now.

"Bad, innit?" he sighted, deflated.

"Mmmmaybe," Price ran the words together, "I think it's, y'know, salvageable."

A glimmer of hope. Tim felt foolish: he knew it showed in his eyes. He was at Andy's mercy here. He felt like a child receiving encouragement from a teacher or relation. "Really?"

what he'd written was entirely terrible. It just wasn't what he'd been aiming for. It lacked direction. But worse than that, it lacked potency. He needed to rewrite – and then some. He also needed a shit. And some food. Which first? Shit or food, shit or food, shit or food? It was all part of the same process: one always ended up as the other, but he went with his gut instincts and took a dump before making himself some toast, spread thickly with Marmite.

Returning to his work, he pondered. Something wasn't right. Not simply with the text, but with him. How come he felt so lousy? How come he felt so agitated?

This is no time for introspection or self-analysis.

But he couldn't help it. The thoughts tumbled from him... thinking his introspection may have resonance, he projected that small fragment of his own psyche onto his character and began to type...

He was in his prime – or at least, he felt he should have been. So was this really as good as it would get? How come he felt so lousy? How come he felt so agitated?

He had the beginnings of a headache building, and so decided that perhaps he should take a break.

"Sure!"

Andy was so assured, Tim found himself veering between an envy-driven loathing and an awed reverence that made him want to hug the guy. *But you don't hug guys... that's just for queers. If you hug a guy you're practically rubbing crotches, it's practically just a step away from sex...* he felt a pulsating in his groin and shifted his gaze away from Price's Adam's apple, the throbbing was just his hangover dissipating...

"You got this on your comp?" Andy was asking.

"Here," replied Tim wearily, offering up a USB memory stick.

"Cool." Andy took the stick and shoved it into the slot. "Leave it with me. Give me ten, twenty minutes. Any chance of a coffee?"

"Yeah," Tim nodded like an eager puppy and headed off to the vending machine.

He didn't usually drink coffee himself – it didn't seem to agree with him – but he felt like shit and certainly needed something by way of a pick-me-up.

Walking back down the office clutching a pair of plastic cups three-quarters full of nondescript grey fluid, he passed a gaggle of lardy older women talking about aquaerobics and

Some fresh air, maybe, to clear his head, to clear his mind. Or maybe another coffee was what he needed... or a tea. Or something stronger. Something to fend off the inevitable hangover. He didn't have the time for a hangover: there was work to be done.

Signing into his emails, he saw a string of spam mails promising a longer, thicker penis and offering discounted viagra.

We know the small secret of your confidence, she does not. Litle help for you, perfect xmas.

Viaaaaaagrrrrrraaa is your magic weapon. A little thing that will contribute to your image of a perfect man. Be healthy and wealthy at this new year.

Make your girlfriend feel happy on celebrate ! No one even know of your small secret of being perfect in bed.

A handful pretended to be important information from his bank, despite not holding an account with any of the banks in question.

Ignoring the one from his publisher, Ant signed out and switched off the computer. He was getting low on milk, and this gave him he perfect

how their "bits are under water and they all go all over and it feels really funny like." The mental image turned his stomach.

"A wrap's 4.5 points! You're better off having one of them full meals with the chicken because they're only 5 – but you don't get much, so you have to bulk it up with some extra vegetables. And the spaghetti on toast's really good for breakfast, you just stick it in the microwave."

How he abhorred these tedious women, the admin assistants and PAs. Not all the PAs were tedious or hounds, of course. Some of the secretaries were worth a squirt, too. And then there was Sindy on reception....

He returned to his desk and passed one of the cups to Andy.

"How's it going?" he asked.

"Yeah, not bad. You'll have a passable report ahead of your deadline."

Tim's relief was palpable.

"I owe you one, mate," he said.

"Too right," Andy honked.

Tim felt like shit, but knew he had a considerable debt of more than gratitude to his colleague here.

The chances were he owed his job to him after this. Not that he was going to admit that, even to himself.

excuse to take a walk, to get some air, to clear his head and maybe – just maybe – get some much-needed perspective.

Standing behind him in the queue to be served, three lardy older women were talking about aquaerobics and how their "bits are under water and they all go all over and it feels really funny like."

Fed up of the food discussion – "A wrap's 4.5 points! You're better off having one of them full meals with the chicken because they're only 5 – but you don't get much, so you have to bulk it up with some extra vegetables. And the spaghetti on toast's really good for breakfast, you just stick it in the microwave" – he switched queues. How he abhorred these vacuous, self-obsessed middle-aged cunts. But middle-aged or not, vacuous, self-obsessed cunts were everywhere.

Outside, two men in suits are lighting up cigarettes. One of them is scrawny and looks gaunt, haunted, the other has a more positive demeanour. He exhales the smoke high into the air, and speaks loudly, an aura of confidence surrounding his perfectly maintained coiffure.

"I mean the fact remains that no one gives a shit about their work, everybody hates their job, I hate my

And while his instinct was to throw out every excuse he could possibly think of – his hangover and the fact he desperately wanted to knuckle down to some work and then knock off early to get home to Amy – he found himself opening his mouth and agreeing.

"Sure. I could use a beer. Hair of the dog and all that," he nodded with an uncomfortable smile.

Less than an hour later, they were propping up the bar, pints in hand.

"I'm resourceful," Price is saying. "I'm creative, I'm young, unscrupulous, highly motivated, highly skilled. In essence what I'm saying is that I'm as *asset*."

Tim felt like anything but an asset as he nursed his extra cold Foster's and forced an air of false bravado. He was in his prime – or at least, he felt he should have been. So was this really as good as it would get? How come he felt so lousy? How come he felt so agitated?

Andy was still talking: in fact, it had been pretty close to a monologue from the moment they set foot in the joint. Tim didn't really mind. He wasn't in the mood for saying much anyway. "I mean the fact remains that no one gives a shit about their work,

job, you've told me you hate yours."

Tone was reminded of an exchange he had had with Simon, back in the days when he too had been a slave to the corporate grind. It had been a disastrous and relatively short career, the memories of which were all too painful for him to dredge up now. He felt lousy, he felt agitated, he felt disappointed with himself and at odds with the world.

Returning home and brewing a mug of tea, he idly scanned a few profiles on MySpace, which only served to reaffirm these feelings of alienation, of separation.

Names Stephanie, Livin In Torquay Moved From South London Few Years Ago. Go To College Bit Shit But Gotta B Done. Work Ina Criminal Defence Solicitors, Hoping Thats Wat Ill B Doin When Im Older.

Enjoy Smokin D Ganja, Drinkin, Music; Espec DnB, Goin Out, Watchin Films And Goin On Camfrog. Love All Me Fam And Friends.

The weekend has landed. All that exists now is clubs, drugs, pubs and

everybody hates their job, I hate my job, you've told me you hate yours," Andy was saying.

"I don't hate it," Tim countered wearily, rubbing his eyes with his thumb and forefinger. His skin felt rough and dry, his eyes sensitive and watery. "I just don't particularly love the amount of travel involved, or the deadlines. Or the pressure," he added.

"Ah, see, I thrive on the pressure," his colleague crunked with relish.

"I thought I did... I did..." mused Tim. "I've just got a lot on at the moment..."

"Only one thing for it," Andy boomed. "Another pint!"

Tim was about to decline, cough up some excuse or another, but at that moment a trio of girls entered. Dressed in office attire, but with a definite hint of sluttiness, they caught his eye.

"Of course. My round again, isn't it?"

"If you insist..."

As the pints flowed, Tim became a different person. Eyes on stalks trailing every piece of skirt that passed his line of vision – as the offices began to empty, the quantity of skirt on the premises began to increase rapidly. Andy was shocked by the

parties. I've got 48 hours off from the world, man. I'm gonna blow steam out my head like a screaming kettle, I'm gonna talk cod shit to strangers all night, I'm gonna lose the plot on the dancefloor. The free radicals inside me are freakin', man!

Tonight I'm Jip Travolta, I'm Peter Popper, I'm going to never-never land with my chosen family, man. We're gonna get more spaced out than Neil Armstrong ever did, anything could happen tonight, you know? This could be the best night of my life. I've got 73 quid in my back burner - I'm gonna wax the lot, man! The Milky Bars are on me! Yeah!

Tea simply wasn't strong enough. It was time for a beer.

Sometimes the writing process became all too much. Tony found himself dragged deeper inside, into the psyche now here we go. It was a contrary and confusing situation: to write required observation, interaction, the acquisition of material. For him, ponderance, musing, reading and specific research served only a limited degree of purpose and provided only so much benefit. Ant was an observer,

transformation in the man he knew as being fundamentally conservative, reserved, proper, uptight. More than once he suggested – albeit rather half-heartedly – that Tim slow down, that he perhaps should curb his growing tendency to make lascivious comments to various girls when they came to the bar or when he passed them on the way to the toilet.

"I want that one," said Tim in a second rate 'comedy' voice, pointing to some leggy blonde piece who had just traversed the room to join some friends. Ignoring his co-worker's protestations, he went over to the girl and struck up a conversation to which she seemed strangely complicit. But for Tim, conversation wasn't nearly enough. Tim was on fire. He wanted it like in the movies, wanted it like in the porn he had downloaded on those rare evenings when Amy had gone out, away to visit her family for the weekend. Yes, life is short and love is always over in the morning, but rationale, rhyme and reason pale beside a single kiss...

"My cock's on fire," he whispered into her ear as they left via the side door...

***

and an interactionist to a point, and while writing, for him, required protracted spells of isolation, was a solitary pursuit, when inspiration was lacking, he needed to get out there amongst people, and to eavesdrop, people-watch... *sock it to me.*

But one problem that almost invariably arises from such situations, in which such pickings are abundant is that of information overload. While a strong advocate of social observation as a source of material, Ant often found himself in a whirl, his mind aspin, adrift in a maelstrom of sights and sounds. Yes, the devil is in the detail. But the music is outside. And there's the rub: the endless dichotomy between the practical and tghe theoretical, the perception and the reality. The reality is the Postmodern Condition, the Anxiety of Influence. No escape.... *Paranoia is knowing more than you can use.* And so he feared that time spent in society, among people, was often counter-productive, the details lost in the sea of information, the broad brushstrokes of a scene vigorously portrayed.

Impressionism…   or photorealism? He wanted to convey it all, simultaneously. And so he teetered

Tim was running late. He'd been held up in traffic, and had to get himself and his notes together in time for a meeting in a little over half an hour. Arriving at his desk he dumped the sheaf of print and scribbled notes down on top of the keyboard. Collapsing into his chair and firing up the PC, Tim saw a head appeared above the monitor.

"Alright, mate," the head beamed.

"Not really," Tim snarled.

"No need to bite my head off," the guy said, raising his hands in a gesture of mock surrender. Who the fuck was this wise guy? Well groomed, well-presented in a sharp new pinstripe suit and crisp dazzling white shirt, he exuded an air that said 'dynamic, go-getting and self-assured.' In short, the kind of man Tim aspired to be, pretended to be, tried so desperately to convince himself he was that he even believed it, most of the time....

"I'm sorry," began Tim, hesitantly. He had been about to say, 'I'm sorry, have we been introduced?' but the sharp dressed man swooped in with the speed of the puma.

"Andy Price," he said, flashing a perfect Colgate smile and extending a well-manicured hand. Tim took and shook the hand – a firm, confident handshake – and loathed its

precariously on the artistic tightrope, continually wavering, veering between the intricate and the general, the pulpish and the literary. *Adorno states that pulp has no place in there sphere that is art.* And yet... and yet: Anthony located his work within the realms of the postmodern and the avant-garde, and established and respected theoreticians such as Jameson contend that the postmodern and the avant-gardes are poles apart and mutually exclusive. But it was Tony's wont to draw on the elements of both the postmodern and the avant-garde, and he positioned himself with the likes of Hutcheon and Skerl who contend that postmodernism is the contemporary avant-garde, suggesting that the parameters now seem to be shifting, allowing for a degree of crossover in which the postmodern avant-garde can exist as a valid period in the evolution of the arts, and to this end postmodern / avant-garde literature can be considered, if not a genre, then a theoretically acceptable mode. Tone not only endeavoured to straddle the boundaries, but to represent the different theoretical frameworks for his own subversive ends.

But as he sat before the PC with his head in his hands, lost in a sea of raw syntax, the emerging text was

owner already. He smelled a rat, sensed a threat.

***

Something was awry. Tim had been walking down this street for what felt like hours, but in truth had probably been a mere matter of minutes. He was convinced he was in Manchester, but none of the accents her heard were Mancunian. Indeed, the Brummie burr seemed to be the dominant dialect. What's more, he had been to Manchester countless times, and knew the city centre reasonably well. But he simply could not place this street he was on now. Of course, it wasn't entirely unfeasible that he had become misplaced, but something was gnawing at him, a feeling that something was not right – not right at all. It's only a feeling... and you should never trust what you feel. But no, something simply wasn't right. He considered asking someone for directions, but thought better of it for fear of looking like a complete imbecile.

Just then, his mobile rang, the incoming call signalled by the Foo Fighters' track 'The Best of You.' He loved that song – it rocked – but he was beginning to tire of its polyphonic

neither postmodern nor avant-garde, and it certainly wasn't subversive. It was simply a mess.

Time to go inside – the cosmonaut of inner space – trawling through the banks of his memory, struggling to find the perfect image, then dissect it, pull it apart, fragment by fragment, teasing apart the fibres one at a time, slowly unravelling a millimetre at a time in order to draw out the minutest of individual details. Was this the essence of literary writing? Did he even want to be a writer if high literary works? Did such writing sit within the framework of his postmodern, avant-garde aspirations? He was torn between his vanity – the vanity that drove his desire to write in a way which would impress the literati, the critics and the establishment with elevated prose, dazzling turns of phrase, astoundingly broad and erudite vocabulary and similarly broad and erudite referencing, the eloquent and careful development of characters and intricately woven plots – and his entirely opposing antagonism toward the establishment, the mainstream, the middlebrow / commercial. These antagonistic tendencies, which, like literary Tourette's compelled him to scribble 'cunt' and 'fuck' at least every other page

yet stunted ring-tone version intruding into his life every five minutes. He took the call without checking the name in the caller display.

"Hello, Tim Watson," he said, adopting his confident, assertive business tone.

It was Amy. "Where are you working today?" she asked.

Tim was perplexed, and a shade annoyed, as we was positive he had told her last night that he would be heading for Manchester in the morning, and that he had an early start, so would be gone before she woke up.

"Manchester," he replied, a little tersely.

"Really?" she sounded surprised.

"Yes, really," he forced back.

"Then why aren't you at the office, and why haven't you been on site yet? I've just had Marcus from your office on the phone saying you weren't answering your phone and that you hadn't shown up. Where are you?"

Tim paused and winced. Winced and paused again. He hedged and cleared his throat.

"Um..." he began nervously. His voice was barely audible: his throat was dry and he felt as though his trachea was contracting, cutting off his

in the most gratuitous fashion, were, he felt, more closely representative of his true desires. But they nevertheless seemed oftentimes to limit the opportunities available to exercise his more 'writerly' tendencies. But no writer worth his salt who doesn't labour to make himself obsolete. As such, he would indulge these nihilistic impulses and fuck the canonical, fuck it till it lay bleeding, comatose, battered, bruised, shredded. Commercial success may be measurable in financial and numerical terms, but artistic success is entirely different: no success like failure. Artistic success can only be truly judged retrospectively and in terms of unquantifiable – even unprovable – measures, such as influence and subsequent development.

Snap out of it! he told himself sternly.

Such terminal procrastination achieves precisely nothing, and the literary merits of a blank page only warrant so much discussion (assuming any publisher would be willing to handle such a text. Besides, the literary equivalent of the blank canvas or John Cage's *4'33"* was merely retreading old ground and as such was of limited artistic currency.

air supply, strangling him from within, his body conspiring against him. The fact of the matter was, he really wasn't so sure. He couldn't even remember the journey. Come to think of it, he couldn't recall parking his car, let alone where.

Snap out of it! he told himself sternly. There had to be a simple explanation. He'd obviously just gone into autopilot, being so very tired after a long week of travelling between different sites and different cities and not sleeping well, even over the weekend.

"Are you still there?" Amy was still on the line. How long had he zoned out for? "Are you alright?" she sounded worried, fretful.

"Yeah, still here," Tim said vaguely. But where was here? The street could have been any street in any large city, and he was unable to find any features that may trigger a sense of recognition.

Snap out of it! he told himself sternly. There had to be a simple explanation. He'd obviously just gone into autopilot, being so very tired after a long week of travelling between different sites and different cities and not sleeping well, even over the weekend.

"Are you still there?" Amy was

It was time. Time to tear everything down, to rip it up and start again. To begin with complete annihilation and commence over, to (re)build from the bottom up. Only complete destruction would suffice.

First, the deletion of the text on the screen. Then, the disassembly of the canon. Cutting up was only the first stage in this process. Ultimately, self-immolation was the objective. Only when there was nothing left could the process *really* begin.

He sat in the empty room, staring vacantly at the blank screen before him. As the dust began to settle, revealing the rubble and ruins of his life scattered and strewn about him, his memories drifted in the dry desert breeze. Listen to the silence, let it ring on... whispering voices, shards of fragmented texts littered the whole imaginary universe, spiralling to infinity through the vortex.

A physiological spasm; seconds to the drop but it feels like the end of the world as we know it. The torn pages flittering down like tickertape caught the new moon on Monday, arriving at the blank canvas, the torn canvas, the autodestructive fuck you to the establishment and the ego. No memory. He sought to run down further, to drain down his memory still on the line. How long had he zoned out for? "Are you alright?" she sounded worried, fretful.

"Yeah, still here," Tim said vaguely. But where was here? The street could have been any street in any large city, and he was unable to find any features that may trigger a sense of recognition.

"So...?" Amy's tone had made a transition from concerned to mildly impatient.

"Yeah, right, sorry," Tim blustered, as he bolted back to some form of reality once again. "I got a bit lost," he explained awkwardly. He hated looking like a cock to anyone, even Amy. Especially Amy. Yes, he wanted to appear – to be – the strong, dependable type, the classic male figure. Not necessarily an alpha male, but the devoted, successful, breadwinning male, the sort of man that women wanted and other men wanted to be. To this end, it didn't do to show any signs of weakness. He couldn't be seen to fail, to let her or anyone down. Didn't want to disappoint. Failure was not an option. It wasn't even in his vocabulary. It was imperative he remained stoic, impervious. Even when he was breaking inside.

"Lost? What, you mean you

banks, to void himself. Obliteration and rebirth.

"No, wait." A voice in the darkness, quiet and clear "The future is written in the past."

"The end is also the beginning," he countered.

But nevertheless, his conscience had been pricked and he paused to survey the ruins, those last remains that had survived the push for total erasure. Now everything must go. And now, sitting alone, on the edge of the precipice: nothing before, nothing behind. A ringing in the air, a voice comes over clear, but he's deaf to it all, he's sick of it all but downs another drink, takes it quick, takes it neat. No escaping the physical world he knows, he's too entrenched and there's no escape so he goes inside again. He begins to type, drawing on the deeper recesses of his memories, his most underground and buried of recollections. Nothing here now but the recordings. No more valuable reference than the mirror, the universal found in the most intensely personal.

He sat in the empty room, staring vacantly at the blank screen before him.

So, who are you? Dredging those deeper recesses proved a fertile source of agony.

took a wrong turn, there was a detour or something? Or it's a different site this week?"

Given his complete inability to recall anything of the journey, it was quite possible he had taken a wrong turn, he supposed. But this didn't go any distance to explaining his extreme disorientation.

"Er, yeah, kinda..." Then, kicking up a gear, opted for the route of spouting brazen bullshit to save face. "The traffic was terrible so I detoured, and came into town another way. 'Cause I was running late, I parked the car in a different place, and I'm just trying to get my bearings. I'll give Marcus a call now and let him know I'm a bit behind schedule." With that, he ended the call and immediately the panic gripped him once again. Lost lost lost... how could it be?

As he wandered the street, up and down, searching for something – anything – a turn off, a corner, a shop, an office, he began to experience a strange sense of déjà-vu. It wasn't that he felt he had been here before, but that he had somehow experienced this moment before. He did not dream often, or particularly vividly, and had no interest in psychobabble or arty-fartyness, the kind of crap spouted by people in floral skirts and baggy

Childhood experiences – schoolyard bullying; various disciplinary experiences, the mental scars of which far outlasted the physical marks; family holidays, complete with the usual ructions, disagreements, tantrums, fallings out, silences, etc., etc.; woodland walks; birdsong; leafy inclines, mossy banks, dappled shade, trickling streams, babbling brooks, ice-covered slopes; the sun sex sand of tranquil beaches rock pools fomenting with life, crustaceans, plankton, anemones... a life in TV.... tracking in slow motion... the image fades to a degenerated sepia.

Flicking through the scenes for that perfect image, that defining moment, that precise snippet of dialogue. The same memories surface, as though there is a glitch in the random repeat function... how random is random? Replay... Over and over and over and over... erase and rewind... Over and over and over and... back and forth, pacing the same rectilinear street over and over and over and over... random? The buildings all looked the same. The road was so, so straight, and apparently never-ending. Was this what it was like to live in a nightmare? The search goes on. Over and over... He felt as though he was losing his mind as he traversed the labyrinth

jumpers – art student tossers and so on – about being in touch with your subconscious and interpreting the meaning of dreams. He simply had no interest. He liked hard fact, solid tangible things, not airy theories and fluffy girly shit. That was not his world, wasn't who he is. But this street had something of a dream-like quality. The buildings all looked the same. The road was so, so straight, and apparently never-ending. Was this what it was like to live in a nightmare? Or had he really driven to Birmingham and become lost in a part of the city he had never been before?

***

That evening, Tim and Amy sat on the sofa watching television. It was the usual mindless ITV evening dross, and with a beer in hand, Tim's mind was elsewhere. Precisely where, it was unclear. Essentially, it was nowhere: he stared vacantly out to sea, his eyes not focused on the gogglebox or even on the plain magnolia wall directly behind it. He was looking at nothing, but rather gazing through, his mind as blank as his expression. It took him a while to even realise he had attained a near vegetable state.

"It's good to just go home and

of his own creation, the text beginning to drift before his eyes as he read it again and again. The text beginning to drift... erase and rewind... Over and over and over and over...

***

Sometimes it's good to enforce a halt. When one finds one's work is becoming a chore, uninspired, forced, it's time to pause. If one is retreading the same ground and repeating oneself, or simply failing to find the words to articulate with the power, potency and clarity which is so vital to conveying that all important essence of life, then to stop, to take time out, to temporarily stop and distance oneself is the only solution. Sometimes this may only require a short breather for a couple of hours, or even a little as half an hour to rest the eyes, for the physical strains of writing are commonly overlooked. On other occasions, a day or so to refresh and reassess is more appropriate. One other occasions still, whole chunks of vital time away from the page is the only way forward. And on other occasions still, there is simply nothing for it but to rip it up and start again. Some pieces are simply not meant to be. This is all a part of the process. Writing is distillation.

chill out, do nothing," he often told those of his friends who were always 'doing' something. Amy concurred. Her perfect evening was one spent simply disengaged in front of the telly. She equally valued long lie-ins: to be up before ten on a weekend was simply wrong. And so they sat, side by side, in silence, the television compensating their lack of sound. The blue light flickered over their faces. Cold, clinical. Dead.

Tim stirred, took a sip from his glass. The lager had become warm and rather flat. He was uncertain how long he had been sitting there like that. Not that it mattered, he told himself. This was his leisure time, to spend as he pleased. He worked hard, and while some – like Andrew Price – liked to play hard, he simply didn't have a taste for that sort of a life. He liked things to be settled, sedate. No alarms and no surprises. Relaxation was his reward. Quality time with Amy.

But there's a voice in the distance, quiet and clear saying something that he never wanted to hear. He tries to shut it out. He wasn't usually given to introspection, but he had recently found himself immersed in what could be described as navel-gazing.

Quality time?

Not only should those moments be condensed and concentrated before being presented in a reduced, more potent and matured form, but also to achieve the desired effect, a large percentage of the materials input at the beginning of the process are lost, evaporated out along the way, before the final product reaches maturity and is ready for consumption. He opened file after file, line upon line, page upon page of text, fragments and entire stories he had written through the years, that he kept stashed in a password-protected folder in a recess of his hard-drive, in search of a paragraph, a sentence, a line, a phrase that would be better suited to his current work in progress. The past rewritten in the present....

I'm numb, can barely move. Can't feel my own body. Don't feel as though this is my own body. Even my own senses feel detached. My eyes are closed. There's light from the lamp, and it filters through the skin of my eyelids which are down over my eyeballs, but I'm not properly aware of that. There are sounds; doors banging next door, cars passing in the street and a car alarm sporadically sounding outside... the wind, the rain, the music playing on the stereo. The Psychedelic

What are you?

Come on, baby,

What are you?

Tim was burning inside. He wanted it like in the movies, wanted it like in the porn he had downloaded and kept stashed in a password-protected folder in a recess of his hard drive. But looking at Amy as she sat on the sofa in her pyjamas he shrivelled inside. Looking at himself as he sat on the sofa, slumped in a jumper and comfort-fit blue jeans – the same cut he had been wearing a decade before, the same cut favoured by sad cunts in their forties who were trying to look a bit cool – he shrivelled inside. So this was his leisure time that he worked so hard for and prized so highly?

He felt his stomach lurch, a sensation like his intestines had just dropped six inches in his abdomen. A darkness.... the bottom would fall out of his world if he admitted that he was in any way dissatisfied with the life he had striven so hard and so long to achieve. But the ennui emanating from Amy was palpable. The ennui he felt within himself was hard to ignore. Even now, Amy's gaze was set on the middle distance, her attention a million miles away. It had been a long time since they had so much as spoken. The television continued rolling out its

Furs are on – 'Book of Days' – but I'm so tired and oblivious it hardly registers on a conscious level. I'm not here, so its effects are subliminal. Yet all of this colours and forms the aural backdrop for my half-awake dreams. I dream I have written everything I have seen, heard, touched, thought and rendered it so perfectly, more vivid than life itself.

The realisation that it was only a dream did not hit until a good few minutes after waking, after he had slowly risen from the depths of slumber, through the flickering light of the mid-levels and the populous shoals of brightly coloured and fast moving thoughts / fish before finally breaking the surface of full wakefulness. This isn't where he wanted to be.

Retreat! Retreat!

No, no retreat and no surrender....

It was no good. Ant's eyes were growing weary and his head was a mess. Time for a break. He flipped off the monitor but left the PC on standby, his document still open. He stood up and stretched his arms out wide. His sternum popped and it felt good. He moved to the living room, and, pouring himself a beer, flicked on the TV.

vacuous drivel... and he was happy.

Also with 2.40, you will be able to check if your friends are online (you'll be able to have up to 100 in your list with the update), read and send messages and change some settings for games, all without having to quit the game you are playing.

While you obviously can't pause an online multiplayer game involving other people, you can rejoin play at any time when you've finished browsing.

As we've reported, 2.40 also delivers trophies to recognise players' achievements in the online arena. Many online games will have gold, silver and bronze trophies – with platinum available for those who bag all three – all displayed on the XMB for everyone to see.

Yes, he was happy.

    The stunted polyphonic version of the Foo Fighters' track 'The Best of You' blasting muffled from the pocket of his jacket, hung on the bottom of the banister brought him back to the here and now with a jolt. Checking the caller display, Tim saw that the number was withheld.

More tech hype shit.

Also with 2.40, you will be able to check if your friends are online (you'll be able to have up to 100 in your list with the update), read and send messages and change some settings for games, all without having to quit the game you are playing.

While you obviously can't pause an online multiplayer game involving other people, you can rejoin play at any time when you've finished browsing.

As we've reported, 2.40 also delivers trophies to recognise players' achievements in the online arena. Many online games will have gold, silver and bronze trophies – with platinum available for those who bag all three – all displayed on the XMB for everyone to see.

    He couldn't concentrate on the television. Ant felt as though his head would explode: pressure, weighing down, drags him to the ground like soaking wet clothes. Reaches for the bottle, this time it's vodka, drinks the long draught down. Then, as if spurred by an adrenaline shot to the heart – not the alcohol, it's not had time to take

"Hello, Tim Watson," he said, making every effort to adopt his confident, assertive business tone and failing miserably. He just sounded tired and nervous.

A crackle, a hum. Static, then silence as the line went dead.

"Tosser," he snarled as he lobbed the instrument down on the arm of the couch.

"'Sup?" asked Amy wearily, looking up for the first time since the phone had rung / looking up for the first time in over an hour.

"Some arsehole with a withheld number just rang and then hung up," Tim snapped, as though it was her fault. He knew he sounded like a cock, but he couldn't help himself. The simple fact was that he had been feeling decidedly fractious lately, and it was difficult to pinpoint the exact reasons why. And because he didn't know, he felt he couldn't really talk about it with Amy – what was there to say?

"Oh," she said blankly and returned her attention to the television. With a sigh, Tim followed suite.

In an instant, 'The Best of You' rattled from his pocket once again. He loved that song – it rocked – but he was beginning to tire of its polyphonic yet stunted ring-tone version intruding

effect yet – he goes to the chest of drawers in the corner of the living room, yanks open the second drawer down, which contains photo albums and box files stuffed with documents and letters, postcards and screes of miscellaneous detritus collected from throughout his life. The solid pine cabinet – inherited from somewhere, he couldn't remember its precise origin – shuddered violently in response to his carelessly vigorous tug. Within seconds, the contents were strewn in various haphazard piles about the room.

He picked a CD from the shelf, more or less at random, threw it into the player ad pumped up the volume. As the treble-heavy, drum-machine driven racket of Big Black's *Atomizer* – reissued on CD as *The Rich Man's Eight-Track Cassette* – assaulted his senses, he rifled the documents scattered about him like a man possessed. Driven by the fast-paced music and a near mania that came from within, Tony began foraging through the artefacts at an increasingly rapid rate. He was driven now, frenzied, as 'Jordan, Minnesota' bled into the tinnitus-inducingly toppy 'Passing Complexion.' He was a man on a mission for something, anything, written on those papers that could

into his life every five minutes.

"What?" he hissed into the handset, microphone just millimetres from his mouth.

"Hey, alright Tim, Marcus here." There was a broad hint of surprise in his voice.

Tim flushed. "Marcus, hi," he said, cringing.

"Tim, hate to land this on you but we've got a bit of a crisis on our hands. Joe's been in a car accident – he's ok but won't be in for a couple of weeks, a bit shaken up, y'know, so we need to cover his site visits for next week. I can email you the details later, but I just wanted to run the outlines by you quickly just now. I know it's late and it's Friday night and that, but..."

By the end of the call, Watson had been briefed on an itinerary that took in visits to Bath on Monday; Stoke on Tuesday; Newcastle on Wednesday, Norwich on Thursday and wrapped up the week with a Friday trip to Sheffield.

Tom slumped on the sofa beside his girlfriend.

"'Sup?" asked Amy wearily, looking up for the first time since the start of Marcus' call.

Tim sat and rubbed his eyes with his thumb and forefinger. His skin felt rough and dry, his eyes sensitive

provide inspiration, or, better still, material he could simply lift wholesale. As for the photographs, some of which were creased and faded, others of which were characterised by the unreal colouring of 1970s commercial film processing, he was looking for a scene or an image that would evoke forgotten events or hint at some kind of potential narrative, fictional or otherwise – *after all, every picture tells a story....*

Glancing over one picture, taken on the last day of his first or second year at secondary school, he's immediately back there. The sun is shining, the faces are all smiling and everything bears the appearance of a happy, carefree childhood idyll. But he knew different.

"Anthony's mum has sex with tramps," Joe had jeered. It wasn't true, but some of the other kids had begun to taunt him about it. "And Anthony's dad isn't his real dad, 'cause his mum's a slag and got pregnant by one of the tramps," Joe had embellished. The rumour that his mother was a tramp-fucking proz and that he was the bastard child of a homeless alcoholic remained with him for a number of years. Children are such shits.

As 'Kerosene' rent the air with ripping guitar nose, there was a knock

and watery. He was exhausted, and this was reflected in his sallow appearance.

He briefly explained the situation and shook his head.

"I'd better make some calls," he said flatly.

He scanned through the numbers stored on his telephone. If he was going to have to cover Joe's work, someone was going to have to cover his. His first call was to Simon. He had company, and seemed rather distracted.

Watson was too fraught and too immersed in his own business to pay much attention to his colleague's distance and lack of focus, although he did find his jocular, almost flippant responses to be a cause of annoyance. He heard a voice in the background at the other end of the line. The tosser had a girl round or something by the sound of it. An inexplicable jealousy tightened Tim's chest. What did it matter to him what Simon did, who he saw? Besides, it was a Friday night, after all...

"..." Simon is talking, although he's getting off track.

"..." Tim is listening. But only half listening: his attention is divided now and his responses are cursory. His thoughts have turned to Sindy. But in his mind's eye, the tape is running a

at the door. Ant ignored it. He had work to do.

"Fuck off," he muttered to himself as 'Kerosene' ended and the battering drum machine of 'Bad Houses' kicked in.

But the knock came again, louder and more persistent this time. Frustrated, Tone rose and cautiously opened the door – there had been some dodgy and brutal incidents in the area in recent months and he wasn't keen on having his head stoved in with a bat so some chav scum could ransack his home and shit in his sink, as had been a recent trend.

It was Simon. And he wasn't alone.

"Evening Tone. Just happened to be in the area – actually I thought I'd drop the CDs round I promised since I had nothing better to do – bumped into Abi on the way," Simon gushed.

"Come in," bowed Tony, hoping his frustration and awkwardness – the former on account of the unexpected and ill-timed interruption, the latter on account of the minor crush he had on the girl who had just landed on his doorstep, who was a mutual friend of his and Simon's – didn't show.

"...it's a great album. But..."

scene in which she's with Simon, right now, and he's thinking it's her voice he can hear in the background.

Immediately, a rage wells up inside him, he can feel his blood pressure increasing, building to a roar in his ears like the sea. Suddenly, Simon's voice seems very distant, like a television just audible through the walls of a terraced house or flat. Why would Sin want a wide boy tosser like Si? Why wasn't she lusting after him? Successful, promotion maybe even to partner in the company in the next couple of years... check the record. He had to kill the call and fast as contradictory and inexplicable emotions rose within him, waves of burning murderous passions. Clenching his fists, he wanted to bludgeon Si with his bare hands, to make him feel pain, and to bleed, a fist hard in the face over and over... and as for Sin, he wanted to use that fist on her too...

Fists of love!

Simon is talking.

"Hmm, I know what you mean." Tony is listening. But all the while, he's making mental notes. If Abi was a character, how would he describe her? How would he use her? *And Simon: how would I portray him? What kind of scenarios would I place him in?*

Feel my hand....

Feel my arm...

Ant's broken out the booze and Abi, though comparatively quiet and clearly a little less than comfortable with her unexpectant host's musical selection – *Feel it!*

Feel it! – is starting to adjust to the situation.

The same can't be said of Anthony, who's beginning to knock it back, and with visible effects. His eyes are becoming glassy, his speech a little slurred.

Fists of love!

Fists of Love!

Fists of Love!

***

Tim woke early to the sound of the alarm. He groaned inwardly. He felt like crap.

Monday morning already? Where had the weekend gone?

***

Anthony woke up feeling rough. He wasn't entirely sure what time his uninvited guests had departed, and had absolutely no idea as to when he'd gone to bed. The evidence was that it

He dressed hurriedly: he had a long drive today. No time to shower, or for breakfast, or to check emails. Tim didn't usually do breakfast anyway, so he was able to bail into the car and be on his way within a matter of minutes. Once on the road, he realised how truly weary he was. No, not weary: bone-tired, fagged out, exhausted, fucked. He flicked on the radio, anything to keep him awake.

"You know when you go to a club you're gonna get searched. Everyone's got knifes, innit."

"Sick... just wrong," Tim muttered to himself. "Used to be able to go out and not worry when I was younger... not like now," he told the radio, overlooking or forgetting the fact that he never went clubbing, then as now.

Half an hour into the journey, Tim began to feel uncomfortable. A grumbling in his intestine, a tightening of the bladder, a sweat broke on his temples. He pulled up at the next service station – the fifteen miles felt like a lifetime – and hovered around momentarily in the lobby while he decided whether to go to the shop first. He hated to be one of those people who just pulled up to services or

had been late – or early, depending on how one looked at it: the light and the radio were both on, a tactic he often employed after a few too many in order to prevent, or at least minimise, room-spin and the vomiting that invariably ensued.

As he attempted to prize his lead-weight head from the pillow, the vox-pops spewing from the radio infiltrated his conscious mind.

"You know when you go to a club you're gonna get searched. Everyone's got knifes, innit."

Riled by the reactionary nature of the coverage – and of the government legislation, and of the response of the average 'man on the street,' Ant rolled over, reached out and hit the off switch.

The previous night began to return to him in small snippets.

In the kitchen, picking cans of beer from the fridge, Abi pops her head over the fridge door.

"Need a hand?" she asks cheerfully.

"Nah, I can manage," he smiles

"Ok, can I trouble you for some ice, if you have any?"

"Sure, no problem."

went into a pub just to use the toilets. But this was verging on pain: a stab shot through his lower abdomen. He wondered if he perhaps didn't need a shit, but elected just to pee, to alleviate the pressure. How he hated public toilets, especially the scratchy bog roll!

He ventured into a cubicle and locked the door behind him. A thin jet of urine, dark brown in colour, spurted from his shrunken penis. Long-term dehydration had withered his bladder, ruined his insides and rendered his complexion sallow. But he failed to notice any of this, he had bigger issues.

His member was nevertheless a disappointment to him. Drooping, dripping in his hand, held between his thumb and forefinger it was a shameful embarrassment: small wonder Amy wasn't busting out of her underwear to get a load of it.

Shaking dry and tucking his trouser minnow away, he pondered over how his sex drive fluctuated so. If only his job wasn't so tiring! But there was something else. Amy. He loved her, yes, of that he was certain, but she was increasingly proving to be something of a personality void. Was he to blame, was he accentuating her tendencies for 'safeness'? Perhaps, at least in part. After all, he never expressed his desires. But how could

"Oh, and where did you say your toilet was? Through here?"

"Yeah, just through there...." he gesticulates.

The conversation was a little strained, didn't flow like it had been in the living room when Simon had also been present. The simple fact was that Tony felt awkward in her presence, and he felt it showed. And the more aware of the awkwardness he became, the more self-conscious he was, fuelling a vicious circle of cringe-inducing jokes and ideas expressed in poorly-structured sentences that collapsed in on themselves. Simon provided a good wall to bounce off and also acted in some sense as a chaperone. But finding himself alone with her in the kitchen, Ant found himself really struggling.

Struggle... his whole life was a struggle, he thought. First, the struggle to fit in... followed by the struggle to achieve, to forge a career... the struggle to survive financially, and the struggle to maintain identity and sanity.

The previous night continued to return to him in small snippets.

In the kitchen, picking cans of beer from the fridge, Abi pops her head over the fridge door.

"Need a hand?" she asks cheerfully. "Nah, I can manage," he

he?

During the time he had been with Amy, it was hard to say precisely how they had grown. Closer? Not really. Apart? Hard to say: they had fallen into the relationship based on some kind of vague notion of attraction. Neither had been in a serious relationship before and so neither really held any specific expectations. And if anything, they had brought out the blandness in one another, the quietness, closedness. After all, neither had been the most outgoing of sorts before they met, and their chance meeting had been a curious and unlikely coincidence at best.

Their relationship had begun tentatively, and had had essentially remained so. Sharing an aversion – terror – of confrontation, bubbling issues were swept under the carpet, and words remained unspoken. Tim would never admit to simmering frustrations or deep-seated feelings of anger or resentment, even to himself, because he couldn't possibly justify them.

He arrived in Chester and completed the survey in no time. The guy the property owners had sent out to liase with him was an annoying little tosser, weedy, lispy, mincey, a stereotypical shirtlifter in a salmon

leers back lecherously.

"Ok, can I trouble you for some ice, if you have any?"

"Sssshuure, no problem," he slurs.

"Oh, and where did you say your toilet was? Through here?"

"Yeah, just through there...."

The conversation was a little strained, didn't flow like it had been in the living room when Simon had also been present. Small wonder, he thought.

His bladder was beginning to throb and his kidneys ached. He girded his loins and gingerly swung his legs out of bed and onto the floor, made his way to the toilet and pissed like a horse.

He's feeling like car crash and wondering why he does this to himself, why he's such a fuck up sometimes, why he simply doesn't seem able to cope with certain things, certain scenarios, certain people. He curses himself for his weakness. Thoughts are streaming through his mind once again.

"Stop staring at her tits, there's no need to be quite so obvious," Simon is saying.

Car crash... car crash...

Perhaps that's what he needs. Forget the mundane situations, the pink shirt. He hated that sort. Fucking ponces. They made him cringe, made him clench his fists and fight back uncharacteristically violent impulses. He'd have quiet happily pushed this irritating little prick off the top of the roof, but his rational side prevented him. He had no desire to go to jail, especially not for such a non-person. Besides, he wasn't a violent man by nature and preferred to express his masculinity in other ways. Fast cars, watching sport, drinking beer, they all proved that he was a real man. Not like the specimen who was currently showing him the store-room and the office to the warehouse adjacent to the main commercial premises he's just surveyed. The thought of two blokes together made him shudder.

"The only way you'd get me near someone's arse is when I'm taking a bird from behind," he'd said on more than one occasion down the pub.

"Or when you're sucking up to the boss!" Andy Price had once cajoled in response.

Tim had resented this jibe deeply, the insinuation that he was some kind of queer would have stung enough without calling him a suck-up. He'd not spoken to Andy for a good week or so after that: he felt that Price

introspective internal monologues, the inner turmoils in which characters wrestle with their fears and the contradictions embedded within their psyches, grown men coming to terms with the long-term effects of childhood traumas, homophobes in deep denial over their own latent homosexuality, seemingly normal individuals wrestling with their darker impulses... forget it. To hell with emotional depth, it was so passé, so fucking *Dawson's Creak*. As Michael Bracewell had noted in his densely-written early retrospective of the decade, *When Surface Was Depth: Death by Cappuccino and Other Reflections on Music and Culture in the 1990's* (2002), during the 1990s appearance was everything – even more than it had been during the yuppie explosion of the 1980s. But the new millennium brought with it an even deeper ennui. Surface wasn't the new depth: depth was entirely dead.

After all, depth doesn't always translate into a page-turner. Casual readers will most likely find themselves pulled under while trying to decipher the author's overeducated jargon and I've-seen-it-all cadence. Who wants that? Page-turning, white-knuckle action is where it's at. The CSI generation may pretend they're

had shown himself to be the obnoxious, offensive prick Watson had suspected when he first met him.

Tim had shoved the table forward and risen sharply. Price had been taken off guard and looked surprised. The two men were of comparable height, and Watson was slight of build, and looked positively waif-like in comparison to his colleague's stockier build. Nevertheless, Price was clearly shitting himself when Watson leaned across the table and took him roughly by the shirt collars, pulling his face close to his own.

"You'd better watch your fucking mouth," he hissed threateningly.

"I... I didn't mean anything by it," Price quivered as he clocked Watson's clenched fist drawing back menacingly. The last thing he wanted was a broken face. Tim was clearly a psycho and Andy realised that this guy should be shown respect.

"You fucking better not, or your nose will be ploughed so far down your throat you'll be sniffing your own arse," Watson snarled menacingly.

A look of terror covered Price's face, and, satisfied he had done enough, Tim threw him roughly back

clever. The viewers like the fact that they can feel smart as they piece together the clues, despite the broad hints dropped through the conversations and *de rigueur* flashbacks. They also like the hint of danger that fiction based on real-life crime carries with it.

Ant pondered this for a moment. The flashback was integral to the storytelling in CSI. Regressive plot development, versions – the same scene retold from different perspectives or revised in the light of new information, new revelations made by the evidence. Faith in science. Science as the new religion. Of course, this narrative method owed much to Tarantino's early films, *Reservoir Dogs* and *Pulp Fiction*. In combination with the clever camera-work – the close-up shots of bullets entering flesh, the CGI recreations of hearts puncturing and lungs filling with blood, this was a different and altogether new sort of action, that when used in combination with scenes of car crashes, flaming buildings, punch-ups, shoot-outs, stabbings, blood, sex and violence made for a holistic experience. He knew what was required to bring his own narrative to life. Yes, detail. Yes, 'fact.' Yes, a 'real-life' element. But above all, what

into his seat.

"Just fucking watch it, alright?" he threatened.

If only... Tim had replayed the scene a thousand times. If only he'd had the nerve! Instead he had sat and fumed, humiliated.

Riled up by the ponce he had encountered while conducting his survey, this scene ran through his mind once more. He clenched his fists, his knuckles white as he gripped his steering wheel *hard*. He put the pedal to the metal and only just avoided a handful of speed cameras as he drove back to the office at an excessive speed.

He weaved into the office, drawn, fraught, fatigued, fucked. He booted up the PC: the newly-installed networked version of Microsoft® Windows© took an age to load. He logged into his emails. His inbox was bursting. Not a great deal of interest: he yawned at the line upon line of circulars from Head Office and from his immediate manager (posted of course, via his secretary). About half of them he deleted straight away without opening. Those from Head Office were invariably completely irrelevant to him anyway. Those from

was needed was ACTION!

But what the fuck did he know about all that sort of shit? First hand, little to nothing, and he knew he struggled to write credibly about matters of which he had such limited experience. It was all over the television anyway. Where was the depth? He idly trawled the Internet, surfing without aim. Anything that caught his eye may prove useful, may provide material. After all, what does any writer do but rearrange the words at his disposal? As Harold Bloom wrote in his seminal text, *The Anxiety of Influence*, 'weaker talents idealize; figures of capable imagination appropriate for themselves.'

This is all very well, thought Ant, *but I can't simply plagiarise large slabs of text*. Moreover, the idea of simply rewriting or editing from existing texts didn't really appeal either. No, he was determined to write his 'own' story if it killed him. And the way he was feeling, he feared it was possible that it might. He felt like train crash and wondered why he did this to himself, why he was such a fuck up sometimes.

Flustered and unable to focus, he absent-mindedly typed in the oft-spoken adage beloved of writers, 'write what you know' into his

Nigel, his manager, were rarely better, being choc-full of corporate bollocks and acronym-laden piffle. The mail entitled 'Q2 Review / Scorecard and Objectives' was a typical example, closing as it did with some meaningless horseshit.

It was a very valuable lesson in what can be achieved when everyone buys into the goal and works together.

He groaned inwardly and deleted the missive, along with a number of others he'd only skim-read. He didn't see the point and couldn't be arsed.

Things had been so very different earlier on in his career. Time was when Tim had been highly motivated and enthusiastic, with ambitions of being made a partner in the company. He'd had the aptitude, the drive, the desire. He didn't simply want a job, he had wanted a *career*. And more than that, he had wanted the status, the kudos, the admiration that comes with success. Yes, he wanted it all: the nice job nice life nice wife nice car nice house foreign holidays twice annually sharp suits expensive shirts designer cufflinks. And why not? If he was going to put the hours in, he wanted to reap the rewards, to pull up

search engine of choice.

Unimpressed by the plethora of 'advice for writers' pages, he resorted to Google for the same search.

Write what you know.

You don't have to know everything there is to know about a given subject before you sit down to write, but meandering and poking around is not entertaining or informative reading. You need a strong grasp on the main aspects of your subject to write about it well. (I'm not saying that you can't write intelligently ABOUT your learning process, just that you can't write compellingly DURING your learning process.)

The reason critics point to authors' first novels as autobiographical is that, to a large extent, when they write about their own lives and the people and circumstances in it, novice authors write well. They might have written three or four books before they got published, but when they wrote from their own point of view, they finally hit the mark.

Creating characters and places from people you know is the best way to write believably, even if you're creating a whole new world writing science fiction. –

to country pubs in a sleek convertible and step out in some neat duds and turn heads. The men would bristle with envy and the chicks would go moist knowing that the man before them was a success, so fuck you. So what if a flash car was considered by some to be a penis extension? Fuck them and their petty jealousies. He'd earned it. And so what if some considered a smart suit and a nice house 'showing off'? Again, he'd earned it and it was his right to wear his achievements for all to see. The suit was a status symbol. The watch was a status symbol. The house, the car, the attractive blonde girlfriend...

But things were different now. His motivation had fallen away in recent months. And having maintained a prominent profile with the directors for some time and made all the right moves and all the right noises, he was no longer the Golden Boy now that Price was on the scene. Tim was highly competitive by nature, but Andy Price was in a different league altogether. For this, Tim admired him and loathed him, feared him even, in equal measure.

Price was the man Watson aspired to be, but would never be. He simply lacked that killer instinct and that natural confidence that flowed so

Ant was unsure of Melanie Spiller's observations and moved on.

Note: I personally am not a big fan of research. It's way to time consuming. And in this business, the faster you complete your project the faster you can concentrate on more money making activities. -

- from *Write What You Know And The Money Will Flow* by Shawn Joseph

...and the more typing gaffes and crappily-structured sentences you'll have, Tony thought to himself. Joseph was clearly a fiscally-motivated cunt and at odds with Ant's art-based principles.

He pondered his past, and also his friends, past and present, for inspiration.

Things ain't cooking in my kitchen, he thought, and decided it was time to take a walk. He picked up his coat and keys, and also his packet of cigarettes and lighter from the sideboard. While he rarely smoked any more, sometimes the situation required it, and this was one such situation. Rather than finding that the deadline spurred him on and provided motivation to plough on relentlessly,

freely from Andy's pores, where only nervous sweat trickled from Tim's. Tim angled much of the blame for his falling from promotion contention and the slowing of his career in Andy's direction – after all, he had appeared on the scene and stolen his thunder – but, while it pained him to admit it, he knew there was something more, something closer to home and deeper inside. That something more was something he didn't want to consider, didn't want to address, certainly not now and preferably not ever. He couldn't think straight in the present: a creeping anxiety was having stagnating effect on his rational thought processes.

Having emptied the contents of his inbox and fired off a few brief replies to the most important emails, Tim dropped some files off with Andy then headed straight home with the excuse that he'd had a long and taxing drive, a difficult survey and that he wanted to make a good start on the report which had a tight deadline. Besides, he had another early start tomorrow.

He checked the name on the incoming call. It was Amy. He knew almost instinctively that it would have been her ringing.

"Hi, Ames," he said, half

he was finding that the creeping anxiety was having a stifling effect on his writing abilities.

Lighting up, he locked the door and headed down the street, uncertain of his destination. Living in Broomhill, he had a number of options. One was to cut just a few streets to Fulwood Road: there was a small cluster of shops that included some charity shops that had, in the past, provided some rich pickings, as well as Record Collector, which, while not exactly bargain basement, carried an impressive selection of new and second-hand titles on both CD and vinyl. But Ant's coffers were empty, and rifling music stock he couldn't afford would only serve to depress him further and remind him of how skint he was. And so he elected to simply walk, and walk. Joining Westbourne Road and then following it on to the point at which it joined Brocco Bank, he made his way to Eccleshall Road. There wasn't really all that much there of interest to him – not since the little independent record shop had closed some years ago – but that was a good thing under the circumstances. Without the temptation to spend, the only expense would be boot leather and calories.

Drawing deeply on his second

sighing, half croaking, his voice cracked with fatigue.

"Hey," she chirruped back.

"Hey," he echoed back, as he commonly did. It bought time, breathing space, signalled to her that he was listening, like a call-and-response of 'Copy,' 'Roger.'

"I was just wondering what time you'd be home for tea tonight," she said in her usual even, gentle tone.

"Um, I'm not really sure," he stumbled.

"Are you ok?" she asked, detecting the uneasiness in his voice.

"Yeah," he said taughtly, attempting to feign a breezy affable tone. "I can't really talk now," he explained. I'm driving and I'm not on my hands free."

"Oh!" Amy's surprise was genuine and uncontained. Tim was always so responsible when it came to driving, never used his mobile without the hands-free kit, never touched a drop of alcohol within a couple of hours of driving and sometimes even refused a beer the night before if he had an early start the following morning. This was out of character. But then, so much of Tim's behaviour in recent days and perhaps even weeks had been rather out of character. It wasn't so much the fact he was distant

cigarette, he felt the nicotine rush. It had been longer than he had realised since he had last smoked and the sensation felt strange. He was wired now as he walked purposefully past the shops and offices in the direction of the train station with no obvious reason other than to keep himself in motion. Stopping, he feared, may bring disastrous consequences, consequences he couldn't conceive or imagine. Moving, however, improved his circulation and the flow of blood around his body and his brain. He invariably got his best ideas when walking or pissing.

The wind was picking up and the sky was overcast, but the air was a bearable temperature: maintaining a reasonable pace, he wouldn't have been cold without his jacket, but nor was he too hot.

He's back in his youth, a scene from one of the photographs he had scattered about the living room floor the night before.

A gentle breeze brushed up through the grass as he sat on the elevated ground and surveyed the land below; the lakes, the village, the trees. A heat haze shimmered the horizon and blurred the vanishing point between lush green land and perfect blue sky. There wasn't a sound to be

– he was often given to being somewhat inattentive when under stress at work – but the extent of his vagueness was becoming hard to deal with. That he had been so vague concerning his whereabouts in the past few days was deeply concerning. Then there was his drinking. He often had a couple of cans after work, and that was never an issue, although she had nagged him about it on a handful of occasions. But these past few nights he had been consuming a four pack, sometimes more. And then there was the night when he hadn't even come home and appeared to have gone out and got absolutely wasted... where had he been? Who had he been with? He seemed to genuinely have no recollection, but her suspicions were aroused. Tim was very good at bottling things up, so when this situation presented itself, Amy simply didn't know what to think.

And so the call ended, abruptly. Amy couldn't help but picture the scene from a road safety advertisement in which a husband was speaking to his wife on his mobile phone while driving, and distracted, collides with another car with a loud deadened thud. The final shot sees him still, a trickle of blood running from his nostril.

Tim's desperate to get home,

heard save for the occasional bird calling and the whisper of the breeze. A cloudless sky, bright and blue, the sun a yellow ball of fire burning down, the image so perfect it's hard to tell if this recollection is real or simply a false memory constructed from an archetype, a film, a picture, a photograph, a postcard. A solitary aeroplane traverses the sky, so high above the earth as to be silent, and almost invisible for the occasional glint of sun reflecting on its metallic exterior. The contrail extends long behind it, undisturbed due to the complete lack of a prevailing wind at any level between the ground and the lower levels of the atmosphere, cutting the sky with a sharp, clean white line in its wake. Such sights used to be a source of utter wonderment and awe, in a time before fossil fuel emissions, greenhouse gasses, pollution and global warming had become common currency.

Carried away on this reverie, he had walked past the point at which Eccleshall Road becomes Moore Street, and was now at the first roundabout. The traffic was heavy: the traffic was always heavy here. There were still a fair few pedestrians, too: mothers with children and pushchairs, walking two abreast while smoking

take off his work clothes and his shoes, which were clammy with perspiration. He wants nothing more than to take a shower, wash away the stress and grime of the day, to tuck into his dinner and drink the long draught down on a cool beer. He wanted to regain the sense of order in his life, and to experience something approximating peace, in the comfort of his own home. But there was something else, inside, pushing him, pushing him, pushing him, pushing him...

He put the pedal to the metal and accelerated with a roar of the engine. He turned off at the next exit – a small B-road – and floored it. He needed to feel the open road, needed to feel the space, the power, the freedom – and at the same time relished the sense of being in control of the machine that throbbed at his command.

As the metal pulsated about his being, he began to feel alive, liberated, masculine. He felt masterful, confident. He felt the blood rush through his capillaries, down toward his groin and within moments he was pitching a tent in his trousers. He open road beckoned him: away from the motorway, the traffic had all but evaporated, nothing ahead and nothing behind. His pulse quickened, he had a

cigarettes and cackling into their mobiles while completely ignoring their bawling offspring as they choked on packets of crisps.

Electing to make his walk a circular, Anthony headed up Eyre Street toward Arundel Gate. Usually, he hated the busy shopping district in the town centre, but concluded that the sights and people he was likely to observe, in combination with the continued movement, may just prove fertile, may just provide that something he so desperately sought, so desperately needed. He cut past the Crucible Theatre, before taking a left and joining High Street before it morphed into Church Street. There had been substantial redevelopment in this part of the city as it had struggled to recover in the wake of the construction of the out of town Meadowhall Centre.

Everything's the same, but different: he's looking with fresh eyes. The Virgin megastore is now Zavvi and sells vinyl LPs downstairs. It used to sell 7" singles, but stopped again without warning. HMV removed its stock of 7" vinyl to accommodate Christmas stock a year or two back and it never returned. Heading on past the City Hall and the fountains, which were turned off for maintenance – they seemed to be off more than they were

need for speed and he inched a little more pressure onto the accelerator, eased on a little more gas, nudged the speedometer up a fraction at a time, rammed the stereo up full tilt – sometimes there was nothing better than some pulsating dance music to take him to another place.

It was exhilarating. Yes! He was alive! He loved to drive. It was one of those perfect experiences that was almost impossible to explain, because it was such a solitary pursuit.

His gristle was throbbing now, and he wanted it like in the movies, wanted it like in the porn he had downloaded on those rare evenings when Amy had gone out, away to visit her family for the weekend. But no, this was better than sex, he thought as his staff strained at the fabric of his underpants and thrust against his fly. He's touching on 90 miles per hour now and he knows he shouldn't go beyond that: if he got caught he'd lose his license. He's close to shooting his load when he spots a van up ahead. He applies the brakes, and he's back to a more sensible 55 by the time he draws up behind it at the next bend.

His horn subsides and he continues the rest of his journey home inside the speed limit and without event.

on – he reached the top of West Street. Fopp had closed after going into administration, and had been replaced by a Costa Coffee. *It could have been worse*, he mused – *it could have been a Starbucks*.

He hated these clone buildings, which were often modern prefabricated monstrosities composed of concrete and corrugated iron, and as uninspiring as the clone interiors they contained. Everything blurs together after a while.... one Starbucks much resembles another and the mediocre fare they churn out much resembles not only every other Starbucks, but more or less very other coffee emporium globally. Supposedly such homogenisation was intended to be somehow comforting: one could stop off anywhere in the global village and know what they were going to get, an international home from home. He'd done coffee shops in the past, killed a few hours and read while consuming more coffee than is sensible, raising his pulse to a dangerous level.

He's too much unchannelled energy as it is, so coffee is the last thing he needs. Alcohol may have the necessary sedative effect, and as he's just passing the Frog and Parrot, just a few doors down from where Fopp was, and decides to stop off for a pint.

***   ***

Before he knows it, he's three cans down and another evening's halfway to having evaporated and he's nothing to show for it. The television's on and it's 'Street Wars' or 'Neighbours at War' or 'Death on Our Streets' or 'CCTV Cities' and Amy's on the phone to her sister and almost without realising, Tim's attained a near vegetable state. He wants another beer, but he's had the last can. He stands up, puts on his shoes and coat and tells Amy he's just nipping to the shop. She covers the receiver with her hand and nods to indicate her comprehension.

Tim doesn't make it as far as the shop. Passing the pub, he glances through the window enviously at the people inside. He rarely goes out anyway, and never drinks alone. That's the domain of sad losers and alcoholics, the sort of objectionable red-faced wifebeaters who prop up the bar night after night complaining to anyone within earshot about how their wife doesn't understand him.

But tonight he feels like his girlfriend doesn't understand him, and so he goes inside.

A beefy woman walks in and sits down with some bloke, probably her partner. She looks significantly

Before he knows it, he's three pints down and heading over to The Grapes on Trippet Lane. He'd received a text from Matt saying that there was a band on that may be of interest, and that he'd be there from about eight. There wasn't much point arriving at The Grapes much before that, as it was closed during the day and was due to open at seven, but it was invariably later. It was a bit of a strange pub, but it put on interesting and unusual bands in the upstairs room, had a good jukebox and an eclectic clientele. It also had a good vibe, and, vitally, good beer.

Having grown weary of the student tossers preening, posing and drinking pissy lager in the Frog, Anthony arrives at The Grapes around 7:30 to find it quiet. He orders a pint of Absolution and takes a seat at a table in the corner of a room to the side. He places his drink down.

He takes a notepad and pen from his pocket and places them on the table in front of him, poised to take note of anything that catches his eye while he's waiting for Matt to show.

A beefy woman walks in and sits down with some bloke, probably her partner. She looks significantly older. She's also stockier, more solid than him, and is clearly in charge. He chomps on some peanuts, swills them down with a glug of Guinness. She chastises him. Yes, she's clearly older, has dimples in her elbows and wears a stupid scarf even though it's bloody boiling.

older. She's also stockier, more solid than him, and is clearly in charge. He chomps on some peanuts, swills them down with a glug of Guinness. She chastises him. Yes, she's clearly older, has dimples in her elbows and wears a stupid scarf even though it's bloody boiling.

He's feeling like car crash and wondering why he does this to himself, why he's such a fuck up sometimes, why he simply doesn't seem able to cope with certain things, certain scenarios, certain people. There's a girl across the bar wearing an impossibly short skirt and a dangerously low top and he can't tell if she's giving him the eye or if he's simply willing her to while he tries hard to look like he's not looking although he knows he's probably staring with his tongue out and a trickle of drool slowly descending from the corner of his mouth.

Cut to the other side of the bar. It's been a difficult day at the agency. Two men are deep in conversation. Their gesticulations indicate a great deal of passionate involvement in their subject matter, and that this is no regular barroom beer and football ramble.

Ant uncaps his pen, flips the cover on the pad and leans forward, trying to catch their conversation.

"Listen."

"Learn from this."

"No-one's listening…"

"Or learning."

"Fuck 'em."

***

***

The days bleed together, and after a week or so, every city merges to become one endless urban mass, grey, uniform: the streets, lined with identical chain stores from Boots and

He's feeling like car crash and wondering why he does this to himself, why he's such a fuck up sometimes, why he simply doesn't seem able to cope with certain things, certain

Superdrug, through HMV and Zavvi, to McDonald's, Starbuck's, Pret a Manger, Burger King, Xerox copies of one another the length and breadth of the country. Tim's just completed yet another survey of yet another anonymous retail hangar, above which 15,000 sq. ft of characterless corporate space stood vacant, its grey walls beginning to flake and the early signs of deterioration through neglect were starting to show.

He's feeling as grey, bland and vacant as this lot. It may be that he's at a crossroads, but he feels more like he's at the end, and it's most definitely a whimper rather than a bang. His heart simply isn't in it any more: in fact, his heart feels dull, deadened, heavy, as though it has turned to clay. He's dead flesh. He looks like dead flesh; pallid, hollow, cracked. He's been here before and knows he'll be here again at some point. Life goes on, and what goes around comes around. He's tired and wants sleep, wants to die. Considers returning to the roof of this cavernous prefabricated monstrosity and tossing himself over the precipice. Decides there's no point, knows he doesn't have the bollocks, that he's a mollusc, knows that's the problem. Hangs his head, closes his folder and heads for the door. A

scenarios, certain people, and why he buckles so easily under pressure.

I sometimes feel that life – or the act of living, and all of the activity that entails, from going to work to cooking and domestic chores, gets in the way of really living. It's so easy to become immersed in the humdrum that you lose sight of the fact that there's so much more... but then I also believe that life lies in the details. It's not about the big things, the grand holidays or the moments that mark significant changes. There are often long spells when nothing happens. That's life. Look closer and there's joy – and pain – and real meaning – to be found in the minutiae. Observing those insignificant fragments, the tiniest shards, the things that fall between the cracks, and appreciating every last one is what life – and writing – is all about.

Ant's in the kitchen, picking cans of beer from the fridge, when Abi pops her head over the fridge door.

The past only exists in some record of it... there are no facts.

How could he trust himself, his own mind? Tony felt like a train crash and his mind was in turmoil.

strange sense of déjà vu. The door closed behind him with a hollow thud.

***

He felt a strange sense of déjà vu as he entered the office. It wasn't his office, the office where he worked and had worked for the last five years, and it wasn't the office he worked in for three years before that. In fact, it was none of the offices he had ever worked in. And yet he couldn't explain this vaguely bewildering sensation any more than he could shake it.

A tall, skinny man with short, mousy hair and an ill-fitting suit that hung from his curved meatless shoulders escorted him to a generously-sized meeting room. The unsettling recognition stayed with him as he took a seat, to which the grey suit man had gesticulated wordlessly, at the long glass table. Another faceless suit, charcoal grey this time, spoke, but while Tim saw his mouth move, he heard no sound. Tim nods. He has no idea why he nods, it's as though he has some involuntary need to nod. Charcoal grey suit moves his mouth silently again. Again, Tim has no idea what he's saying or why he can't hear. He's not even sure if the dude's actually speaking or if he's simply

I'm writing history, he told himself.

***

Another plastic spoon, another coffee, another table routine... He's back in the room and the hallway is moving like the ocean... His head is swimming and he's short of air, opening his mouth and inhaling deeply but his lungs draw no oxygen.

This is what it must feel like to drown, he thought.

He's had similar experiences before, but only in dreams. This time it's real. No, this isn't some kind of metaphor. This is real. Something's wrong. His head's swimming, the people, even the room around him, appear as though in soft focus, and distorted. The sounds are distorted too.

Ant looks down at his hands: he can't feel them. But they're still there, on the end of his arms. He's almost surprised by this. His right hand is holding a pint glass, half full of Absolution. The mid-straw coloured beer with aromas of tropical fruit, particularly mangoes, boasted a strength of 5.3% ABV. Strong, but not sufficient to induce the sensory overload – no, the sensory warping – that Ant was experiencing, even after miming.

Why would he be miming? That doesn't make any sense... Nothing made any sense. *Am I deaf?* The eerie silence, which Tim could only liken to how he expected it might sound like in a soundproof padded cell – something he had never experienced during the course of his extremely normal life – was only one of his concerns. Where was he? Why was he here? Who were these people?

He nods again. It's not even a compulsion. He simply feels himself nodding as though he was a marionette, his actions controlled by some invisible puppeteer.

Charcoal suit man walks stiffly from the room and returns almost immediately with a small plastic cup full of some foul-smelling brown fluid. It could be the pumped contents of someone's stomach for all Tim knows, but he instinctively knows it's coffee.

Tim speaks, no words leave his mouth. Charcoal Suit smiles and nods.

Charcoal Suit walks around the table and sits down opposite. Tim's feeling hemmed in: Baggy Grey Suit is situated at his left elbow and he feels like he's a piece in a game of chess and the moves available to him are diminishing by the moment.

The meeting commences. Tim

five or six pints, and he's only had two or three. Or maybe four. The beer was sweet all the way through, balanced by bitterness at the finish. Flavours were fruity with toffee-apples and bananas. A clean tasting beer, sweetish but not cloying. It was very drinkable. But he was not very drunk, of this he was convinced.

The noise was a muffled roar: the band played on, crammed onto the tiny stage with their instruments. The room was small and Ant was about halfway back between the stage and the mixing desk – which meant that he was about twelve feet away from both. But he felt as though the stage was half a mile away and he couldn't hear the music for the immense sound that filled his head, like an aircraft taking off.

He heads to the lavatories. He knows he'll find no peace in there, but he needs to cool down and he also needs to piss, badly. He takes aim and fires, but an involuntary shudder causes him to piss over the toes of his own boots with a hollow, cardboardy sound. It's time to leave.

***

Around me, the other customers, spragged in a lazy Sunday

finds he's struggling. The trouble was, he didn't really find buildings in themselves all that inspiring, and the suits around him are living and breeething commercial property. There's talk crossing the table, line upon line of factual data and a grasp of figures and certain scientific concepts regarding the deterioration of concrete, the weakening of iron girders, the flammability of certain materials and so on. There are flip charts and flow charts and Microsoft® Office PowerPoint® slideshow presentations.

The presentations were slick. A beefy bloke in a navy pinstripe suit spoke commandingly about the business plan for the forthcoming financial year and the company's 'high-level' strategies.

Some middle-aged bim with goofy teeth and a tasteless trouser-suit is presenting now. She's clearly wise to using Microsoft® Office Fluent™ interface but her presentation is all style and no substance. Tim wants to speak, wants to scream. She goes on for an age, extolling the virtues of 'building relationships,' 'being progressive' and 'proactive cascading.' She's winding down her interim report and the business projections for the next six and 12 months and she's pushing to end with a positive, with

morning manner in the large, deep sofas, their coats and scarves strewn across the backs and arms of the furniture, laugh and smile, hangovers beaten into recession by the caffeine and the traditional coffee-house collation. They either don't know or don't care about the world outside – not in terms of the weather, so much as the everyday agony of existence – and are more than likely simply happy to be indoors and in company and glad that it's Sunday, day of rest.

***

"Look, *I* know I'm not a bad writer, so much as a writer who is making it their objective to write against the grain," Tony's telling Simon. "Arguably, that makes me a writer who is destined to spend their career constantly shooting themselves in the foot and making precisely no money. What it boils down to is that my writing simply doesn't belong: which could be translated as *I* don't belong."

"But you don't," Simon hooted. "You've always been a misfit. And proud of it. I don't see what the problem is." He's kidding. Half kidding, anyway.

Anthony put his usual face on,

some encouragement, with a flourish.

"You're moving it forward, which is good," she yodelled. "You're moving everything forward... which is good."

Everyone sitting around the table nodded earnestly, affording themselves a brief but oh-so-smug smile. A general babble briefly ensued before Charcoal Suit resumed order and began his conclusion.

Only at this juncture did it occur to Tim that he could hear once more, although the corporate piffle floating on the hot air that filled the room made him almost wish that he couldn't. He zoned out again as Pinstripe Suit began his round-up, and so was completely at a loss when he spun a question directly to Tim.

He's feeling like car crash and wondering why he does this to himself, why he's such a fuck up sometimes, why he simply doesn't seem able to cope with certain things, certain scenarios, certain situations.

He has nothing to say, opens his mouth and finds he's still incapable of producing sound. His ears are filled with deadened, indistinct sounds, like his head is under water, a muffled roar. He's short of air, opening his mouth and inhaling deeply but his lungs draw no oxygen.

but was bruised. He knew that his friend spoke the truth. But at the same time, he felt a certain pull. He considered Simon's position, and didn't envy it one iota. As he saw it, Simon had sold out, had become a corporate whore. Sometimes he complained about his job, but he never for a second seriously considered quitting. A slave to capitalism, Simon was forever destined to replicate the circumstances of his alienation. Ant was pleased he had managed to escape the corporate grind. But it hadn't been easy. It had taken something akin to a breakdown to break the cycle. In Simon, he saw elements of his old self: the one desperate to extricate himself from a bad long-term situation, but with no idea how, or even if to do so would necessarily be the wisest course of action.

The difference between himself and his friend was, as Ant constantly reminded Si over pints, that Simon was willing to accept the process, the exchange of time spent doing something thoroughly soul-destroying for money, as a way of life. Tony considered this trade-off to be the big sell-out, and much as he liked and respected his friend, simply could not agree with his position. In return, Simon thought that his friend was an

It's just another day at the office, the same as any other.

***

It was as though the click of the hypnotist's fingers in front of his face had brought him back. He was in a daze, but he saw through his eyes with remarkable and almost blindingly clinical clarity and it didn't look good. Moreover, it looked like nothing he had ever seen, at least not in his own life. It was like a scene from a film or something on TV; he's in a club and the music's pulsating, the lights are strobing and glistening bodies are undulating and writing, serpentine to the thumping mesmeric beat. This is not his scene.

Something inside him had flipped a certain trigger, one he had not been previously aware of. Blinded by lust, he liked them tall girls, he liked them short girls, he liked them brown hair girls, he liked them blonde hair girls, he liked them big girls, he liked them skinny girls...

A gut pull dragged on him: he knew he wasn't himself. A flicker of electrical pulses between the neurones of his hippocampus caused a brief thought of Amy to flash across his mind.

What am I doing? he thought

idealistic bozo for failing to accept that the only way to survive was through labour, and given that manual labour had been superseded by tertiary service-sector industries in contemporary Western society, that meant working in a shop or office or other such job in order to pay the rent – something artistic endeavour alone simply could not do.

"I mean the fact remains that no one gives a shit about their work, everybody hates their job, I hate my job, you've told me you hate yours."

Tone was reminded of an exchange he had had with Simon, back in the days when he too had been a slave to the corporate grind. It had been a disastrous and relative short career, but at least he had acquired a broader perspective on life, and felt able to objectively discus the benefits and disadvantages of regular paid employment and confirming to the model of late capitalist society.

"Precisely. So what's it worth? Everyone's spending almost their entire waking lives doing something they detest, and for what? They're unfulfilled, they're unhappy and they're fixating on earning enough so

to himself. He was so drunk he was dizzy, and he was no longer able to feel his hands. His gums, too, felt numb.

But Tim's on fire and his cock's about to explode. He wants it like in the movies, wants it like in the porn he had downloaded on those rare evenings when Amy had gone out, away to visit her family for the weekend. Yes, life is short and love is always over in the morning, but rationale, rhyme and reason pale beside a single kiss...

The music's relentless, non-stop pulsating dance, not the mainstream chart-dance that many city-centre clubs play but something altogether more intense, more hypnotic. Tim was in a trance, felt like he was swimming, like he was floating, like he was detached from his own body. He desperately wanted to reconnect, with his life, with everything, but simply couldn't find himself, he was floating in space.

Tim wasn't thinking beyond what he wanted as he turned his drunken leer on some bottle-blonde in an impossibly short skirt and dangerously low-cut halter-neck top. He liked the way she put her hands up in the air. He liked the way she shook her hair. He liked the way she moved.

they have a stash for when they retire – assuming they'll have a long and happy retirement, when the chances are they'll die as soon as they get there, if they even do." Ant was just warming up. *"To use the popular jargon, the options are essentially that you can either be cash-rich and time-poor, or time-rich and cash-poor. And as your time may be finite, why put such an arbitrary value on it as money, which in itself has no intrinsic value anyway?"*

If Anthony recalled correctly, this expostulation had yielded a snort and a shrug from Simon.

As he saw it, Si knew that Ant was right but was unwilling to accept when he was beaten.

But Tony had been on a roll and wasn't about to let up.

"As I see it, capitalism's a con. Even late capitalism... the laissez-faire capitalism that came in with Thatcher and has continued thereafter... it's got fuck all to do with personal freedom: it's a tool of oppression, thinly disguised. And what gets me is that people fucking buy it!"

"Of course they do," Si had concurred. *"They see that they can better themselves. And hard work can be rewarded. And there's always something to aspire to. Even those*

He was feeling courageous. He began by dancing close, throwing moves and postures. Soon he was talking to her. She was laughing. Yes! He was really doing this! His cock was on fire. He wanted to grab her by the hair and throw her against the wall... but pace is the trick, he thought, and instead placed a hand on her naked thigh as he went to whisper in her ear...

The shortness of her skirt made for easy access, and her thong was little obstacle as he pushed the crotch aside to reveal her shaven snatch. Drunkenly, she guided his meat into her. He shot his load after a couple of feeble inebriated thrusts.

***

Tim woke early to the sound of the alarm. He groaned inwardly. He felt like crap.

Monday morning already? Where had the weekend gone?

Tim sat and rubbed his eyes with his thumb and forefinger. His skin felt rough and dry, his eyes sensitive and watery. He was exhausted, and this was reflected in his sallow appearance. His cock was on fire and he yawned when the Foo Fighters' track 'The Best of You' rattled from his pocket for the

lower down the ladder can aim for something, and they can make themselves feel good with clothes, cars, cheap package holidays overseas..."

"Can you hear yourself?" Barker had been on the brink of apoplexy. Even though he knew his friend well enough to tell that he was in part playing devil's advocate, he could also tell that he actually believed some of the tripe he was spouting. *"You've got a fucking degree and you're doing admin for an insurance company on a salary that's well below what we're led to believe is a 'graduate wage.' You can't afford to buy a house, you're hardly lashing out on designer duds every few days, where's your cheap package holiday overseas? You're struggling, and you hate your job. So what's the reward? What's the incentive? Early retirement – something else everyone aspires to but no-one in the real world on a normal wage gets? Don't think so. Flash car? You can't afford to run one and take the bus everywhere."*

Simon was accustomed to Anthony's rants, but this one had been something special. And he had been far from done.

"And the fact you're defending the system is proof positive that it's a

umpteenth time that day. He loved that song – it rocked – but he was beginning to tire of its polyphonic yet stunted ring-tone version intruding into his life every five minutes. He killed the call, wasn't about to speak to anyone at this time of the morning, when he wasn't even fully awake. What time was it? The glowing acid-green LCD of the bedside radio-alarm – not that he ever used the radio on it – said 06:05. He was fucked if he was going to speak to anyone at that time of morning. He struggled to manage a mumble in Amy's direction, although the fact she rarely woke up before he left for work made this less of an issue than it may have otherwise been.

He dressed hurriedly: he had to make an early start if he was to complete all of the work he had to clear today. No time to shower, or for breakfast, or to check emails. Tim didn't usually do breakfast anyway, so he was able to bail into the car and be on his way within a matter of minutes. Once on the road, he realised how truly weary he was. No, not weary: bone-tired, fagged out, exhausted, fucked. He flicked on the radio, anything to keep him awake.

Moyles was spouting an endless ream of bollocks on R1. Tim often found himself with Moyles and

conspiracy. The masses have been duped. Similarly, the idea that new technologies have improved our quality of living and the amount of leisure time we all have is completely fallacious. Faster communication equals more communication. There's no escape, you're wired into the system, with mobiles and the Internet. People are so busy chasing their tails and being pressured to deal with all of these phone calls, text messages and emails that they may think it's easier to keep in touch than ever before, but it's quantity, not quality. When was the last time you sent or received an email that was more than, say, three lines long? You've also told me yourself that you don't always get to take a lunch break, or if you do you don't take the full hour you're entitled to because of the amount of work you've got. And why's that?"

Simon had begun to respond, but Tony had cut him off.

"They've laid off so many staff because apparently they're superfluous, redundant in all senses, due to automated systems, electronic communications and so on. But faster communications coupled with increased turnover simply equals more work, not less. And now there are fewer people to actually cover the

his crew of spivs for company in the morning. He wasn't really a fan of Moyles, but thought he had his moments when he was hilariously funny. Tim wasn't in the mood for this brand of humour this morning, though, and he wasn't being particularly funny, instead giving far too much airtime to his self-indulgent opinionated meanderings about nothing much at all.

Stuck in traffic, Tim began to get frustrated. He rummaged around in the glove compartment and dug out a handful of CDs. The Arctic Monkeys' debut was at the top of the pile but he tossed it onto the passenger seat with disinterest. He had soon wearied of their clever observations. He wasn't in the mood for Editors' *The Back Room*, either: simply too depressing. Coldplay, likewise. He plumped for a compilation – *40 Indie Hits* or *Indie Anthems* or *Classic Guitar Indie* or *The Best Indie Album in the World... Ever! Vol 7*. He had a handful of them at home and always kept a couple in the car. They made for good, easy, driving music. Hearing Oasis' 'Wonderwall' took him back a few years and he upped the volume a notch or two and nodded along to 'Naive' by the Kooks, tapping the staring wheel in time with the funk-infused rhythm.

work, so you're effectively working harder and doing more for the same salary – effectively you're being paid one wage to do the work of, what, three people?"

"Probably four," Simon had conceded.

"Right, I think that proves the point. It really is a case of the rich getting richer, etc. the workers – who do the work – get paid the same to do more – much more – which is the equivalent of a pay cut. This of course maximises profits, but those who really achieve those profits don't benefit from them, not really The only ones who really benefit are the top-flight executives and the major shareholders, who are often other companies and the top-flight executives, who of course get more share options and obscene bonuses on top of their already obscene salaries. So everyone gets fucked over and no-one's happy, only they can't admit that they're not happy because it's somehow socially unacceptable to be seen to be dissatisfied, just as it's socially unacceptable to be seen to be poor, which is why everyone has to have the big house nice car overseas holiday labelled clothing, and all the while they're shopping at Netto and Asda but take Sainsbury's and M&S carriers to

He pumped the volume up even higher when 'Living for the Weekend' by Hard-Fi came on and the traffic began to move again. So rarely did a song sum up his life so completely. Yes, this song was his life. This buoyed and depressed him in equal measure. He liked having a soundtrack to his life, that a band had managed to accurately and succinctly encapsulate his existence. He only wished his existence wasn't so mundane.

Still, at least he belonged. And better to belong in the rat-race, rolling along in a mundane, hum-drum existence than to be out on a limb, isolated, standing out like a sore thumb or some kind of freak. *Yes, it's good to rise above the average*, he thought, *to be **better**, but different... no, that just wasn't good. People looked at you strangely. Treated you different. and not in a good way. Like in school, if you're not with the crowd hen you're destined to get endless gyp, bullying... so you have to fit in. And the best way to show them is by playing them at their own game, to do what they do, only better.*

In school of course, it's all about who has the right trainers, the right bag, the right haircut, and who's best at sport, cool things. In adulthood, there's even more at stake. Tim was

put their Netto shopping in, because it's all about image. Most of them won't even admit to themselves that they're unhappy and dissatisfied. They're in denial. So their dissatisfaction, their unhappiness, their anger at the lack of control they have over their situation, over their lives, manifests itself in different and obtuse ways, often not even conscious. They have to inflict pain on others, prove their superiority, through the exertion of small-time power-play... the wife-beater who gets shafted by his boss venting his frustrations when he gets home, loses control at home after he's had a few, feels like he's somehow taking control in a different environment... rapists, racists, homophobes, stalkers, fascists, all taking out their rage on innocent parties because they can't admit to themselves that they're emasculated, weak, fucked over, fucked up..."

This was the world. Anthony knew that he was surrounded by an encroaching darkness.

He cast his mind back to another event, another time in his life completely, a time long ago in a place far away. A time and place he can never return to, isn't sure if it exists now or ever did. Darkness was falling over Tony's life: golden ages were but

torn: half of him felt like an adult, the other still felt like a kid.

***

A gentle wind brushed up through the grass as he sat on the elevated ground and surveyed the land below; the lakes, the village, the trees. Heat haze shimmered the horizon and blurred the vanishing point between lush green land and perfect blue sky. There wasn't a sound to be heard save for the occasional bird calling and the whisper of the breeze.

No responsibility... freedom... life was good. Yes, ignorance was bliss, and he yearned to be back there now, on the holidays of his childhood.

Something strange is beginning to happen. Memories flicker... deep, dark memories, recollections he didn't know he had of people he had forgotten ever meeting, places he had forgotten having been. Scenes began to play as if at random, as though someone had broken into the projector room and was playing archive footage, long lost, at random, digging out reel after reel of film and throwing them in, giving them a spin then changing them. Image upon image, scene after scene in rapid succession, piling up one on top of the other, with no semblance of

a myth, the effects of memory, distorted, rose-tinted by nostalgia. But this was no time for maudlin wallowing, in fact it was no time for anything. His head was a mess, and while he was determined to write his 'own' story, he was beginning to fear that the task might kill him. He felt like train crash and wondered why he did this to himself, why he was such a fuck up sometimes.

Flustered and unable to focus, he returned to flicking through his friends in MySpace and Facebook and checking out the latest news from bands he was interested in, as well as a few others who he had never heard of, but who had sent him friend requests. Anything to avoid the task at hand: he listened to a few of their shittily-recorded piss-poor generic tracks while scanning comments left by 'fans.'

Hello :) I'd jsut liek to say that you're music really beautiful and so different to anything else of heard, and i'm coming to the big chill, so i'll get to see you :)

Depressed, Ant wrestled with the three-way dilemma of tea, coffee or beer. Deciding it was too early for beer and that he needed a boost, elected for a coffee, although more than a pick-

sequence, chronology or order. Not only his life, but everything he had seen, heard or said passed his conscious mind for fractions of a second, an endless flicker of mismatched sounds and images. Disorientated, a sweat broke on his brow. Tim had no idea where he was, and was beginning to lose a grip on the idea of exactly who he was.

It was as much of a miracle as it was a relief when he felt normality seep back into his being, and with perfect timing, too, as he pulled up in the office car park.

He ambled into the office, feeling a little dazed, and fired up his PC. He checked his emails first. His inbox was bursting, with pointless shit mostly. He yawned at the line upon line of circulars from Head Office and from his immediate manager (posted of course, via his secretary) and deleted at least half of them straight away without opening. There were a couple telling him he had received friend requests on MySpace. Tim tended not to really use his MySpace account, couldn't really be arsed with social networking, didn't really have the time, and preferred Facebook when he was in the mood to interact with people he didn't really like and wished he no longer had contact with. Nevertheless,

me-up, he needed rest. He rose from his chair, rubbing his eyes. He headed into the kitchen and fired up the kettle while scooping coffee into his three-cup caffetierre and taking the bag of sugar from the cupboard: he was going to make the strongest, sweetest brew possible.

On returning, he checked out some of the profile details of vacuous bims with big teeth, big tits and bottle-blonde hair who listened to these godawful bands and who associated with their illiterate fans. Just like the bands, they were all the same.

Ant actually quite enjoyed MySpace, and had, in recent months, found social networking – a phenomenon he had been particularly sceptical about – both fun and useful, having made contact with a number of like-minded authors and others who shared, with the same passion, his eclectic and non-mainstream tastes in both music and literature.

But like being out on the street, on a train or working in an office, MySpace was simply another microcosm, containing a broad cross-section of society, albeit on a global scale. As an avowed, self-proclaimed misanthrope – or, perhaps more accurately, a misfit with tastes which lay beyond the fringe of the

he checked out the profiles of those who had sent him the requests. The first was a pretty foxy-looking chick, and at 22, a few years younger than him.

My huge interest is Nails and nail art-im really loving korean nail art at the moment. The designs are so inspiring! I learn something new everyday. I also really enjoy fitness-i try to go to the gym at least three times a week so as to keep healthy. My favorite classes are spin and body pump. I also love the Power Plate which gives fantastic results with the least effort.

Dumb bint, he thought, but accepted the request because there were a couple of suggestive pics in her album.

I would like to meet people who when they know something is wrong have a voice and who are prepared to stand up and say something. People who are non judgemental, have an open mind and who are willing to look at both sides of an issue. People interested in capital punishment would also be a bonus!! x

Tim stroked his chin, pondering that final statement. *Yes, those sick bastards, those paedophiles, should be*

mainstream, and an outlook that corresponded with his tastes – Ant found himself at odds with many of the other users. Nevertheless, it was a fascination he couldn't give up.

My huge interest is Nails and nail art-im really loving korean nail art at the moment. The designs are so inspiring! I learn something new everyday. I also really enjoy fitness-i try to go to the gym at least three times a week so as to keep healthy. My favorite classes are spin and body pump. I also love the Power Plate which gives fantastic results with the least effort.

Riveted, he sipped at his piping hot coffee and scanned another profile. The world weighed heavy...

I would like to meet people who when they know something is wrong have a voice and who are prepared to stand up and say something. People who are non judgemental, have an open mind and who are willing to look at both sides of an issue. People interested in capital punishment would also be a bonus!! x

Ant stroked his chin, pondering that final statement. *Unless she's into extreme sadism and was seeking fucking strung up by the balls and executed in public! Those extremists, terrorists, suicide bombers... Queers, too...* He accepted this invitation too. *And why not?*

There was work to do, but he was in no frame of mind to do it. Tim sat and rubbed his eyes with his thumb and forefinger. His skin felt rough and dry, his eyes sensitive and watery. He was exhausted, and this was reflected in his sallow appearance.

He was in his prime – or at least, he felt he should have been. So was this really as good as it would get? He felt like a car crash, and needed to pull himself together, and fast. He headed over to the coffee machine in the corner of the office and hit the buttons that would yield up the strongest, sweetest brew available.

Returning to his desk, he dumped the sheaf of print and scribbled notes down on top of keyboard. Collapsing into his chair and firing up the PC, Tim saw Andy's head appeared above the monitor.

"Alright, mate?" he beamed.

The traffic begins to move more freely. Tim sensed a change in the lighting in a sky which was dark, threatening, thunderous. At that instant, the sky crack'd – shafts of

willing participants for a snuff movie... no... Everything that is wrong with humanity, encapsulated in a single statement... so succinct... the weight of despair bore down hard and heavy.

There was work to do, but he was in no frame of mind to do it. Tony sat and rubbed his eyes with his thumb and forefinger. His skin felt rough and dry, his eyes sensitive and watery. He was exhausted, and this was reflected in his sallow appearance.

He was in his prime – or at least, he felt he should have been. So was this really as good as it would get? He felt like a train crash, and needed to pull himself together, and fast. He headed into the kitchen and fired up the kettle while scooping coffee into his three-cup caffetierre, then took the bag of sugar from the cupboard: he was going to make the strongest, sweetest brew possible. It didn't seem to help. He wanted time, and he wanted it now.

Hours passed. Or maybe even days.

His mind wandered. He was transported back to his short-lived office career. All the times when he should have been working, but he really couldn't be arsed. Long afternoons – and mornings – spent,

golden light beamed down from the dark clouds, their edges illuminated, glowing – radiating, reaching down to the earth...

He had no surveying to do today: he had a number of reports to write up, more phone calls to make than he cared to contemplate, and, worst of all, a meeting in the boardroom with the company executives up from London, along with a number of representatives from other regional offices which was scheduled to run from 9am through to midday. It was a chunk he could ill afford to take out of his busy working day – just another day at the office.

On arrival at the office, Tim fired up his PC. The text was beginning to drift before his eyes as he read it again and again.

His mind wandered. Tim found himself fantasising about Amy in her powder-blue pyjamas, scenarios in which he had thrown the curtains open and pressed her against the window as he took her from behind... his divided self collided and he saw it was in fact Sindy he was sticking his cock into. He glanced down to change gear and realised he had a monster boner. He'd have to deal with that sooner or later. He had some Tesco mansize facial tissues in the back sea... but no, not

squandered slacking off and dreaming of doing something else, anything else.

His manager had been a cunt. And a bitter one at that, and he only stuck it out at the Council because it was a safe job where they weren't too strict, making it easy to toss it off. And toss it off they did. Sometimes he engaged other members of the team in fairly conventional hijinks, such as throwing paper balls at one another or Sellotaping the mouthpiece up on someone's phone. Others, they'd get creative, anonymously sending the most random objects to unsuspecting members of staff in other departments. Their greatest achievement to date was dispatching a whole melon to Kev in Finance. But more often than not, he just tossed it off, plain and simple, emailing his mates, surfing the net and dicking about doing whatever came to mind. The experience invoked dark thoughts even now.

The darkness was not only Tony's perception, but real. Outside, the sky was dark, threatening, thunderous. He looked up from the screen and out of the window.

At that instant, the sky crack'd – shafts of golden light beamed down from the dark clouds, their edges illuminated, glowing, radiating, reaching down to the earth... divine

now. There was work to be done.

He accelerated onwards as the traffic flowed more freely, escaping the gridlock and the feelings of enclosure, which had bordered on claustrophobia while he had been hemmed in between vehicles jammed end to end, bumper to bumper. He felt liberated, as though a weight had been lifted.

***

Do you ever feel that there must be something more?

First of all I have a great love for Jesus Christ, it is all because of Him that we are alive! If you don't know Him personally I strongly encourage you to get to know Him. God is good, He is Just, He is awesome, and He loves you! He is coming back soon and hell is a horrible place, you don't want to go there. My family is very important to me and out of all of them, I love my mom the most!!! I have a great brother, Jonathan, who faught for us all in Iraq for 2 yrs, so many have lost their lives. Praise God my brother came home! He is doing real well and living near Alamosa with his girlfriend Balinda, he has one son, Jonathan Trueblood who is 10 and doing well also.

inspiration?

His typing pace quickened as the thoughts flowed through him more freely, as though a dam had burst and the floodwaters were beginning to engulf the dry valley. Feeling the sea change, feeling liberated, he accelerated on toward the end of the text. It was as though a weight had been lifted.

***

A cloudless sky, bright and blue, the sun a yellow ball of fire burning down, the image so perfect it's hard to tell if this recollection is real or simply a false memory constructed from an archetype, a film, a picture, a photograph, a postcard. A solitary aeroplane traverses the sky, so high above the earth as to be silent, and almost invisible for the occasional glint of sun reflecting on its metallic exterior. The contrail extends long behind it, undisturbed due to the complete lack of a prevailing wind at any level between the ground and the lower levels of the atmosphere, cutting the sky with a sharp, clean white line in its wake.

A gentle breeze brushed up through the grass as he sat on the elevated ground and surveyed the land

Returning to his desk, he dumped the sheaf of print and scribbled notes down on top of keyboard. Collapsing into his chair and firing up the PC, Tim saw Andy's head appeared above the monitor.

"Hi, Andy," he said, half sighing, half croaking, his voice cracked with fatigue.

Replay... Over and over and over and over...

"Are you still there?"

"Hey..." he croaked. Tied to his mother's apron strings, he winced with embarrassment.

He felt like a car crash. "I, look, I have to go," he cut her short. "Got to get to work. I'm seriously fucked up."

Yesterday...   today... tomorrow...

I think I've fucked up. I've got to get this report in by 2pm and I'm struggling.

Andy's head appeared above the monitor. He felt his sphincter pucker. Tim cast his eye over the others who worked there. His mind wandered.

"Stop staring at her tits, there's no need to be quite so obvious," Simon is saying.

It was Amy. His blood ran cold. Confused, flustered and feeling

below; the lakes, the village, the trees. A heat haze shimmered the horizon and blurred the vanishing point between lush green land and perfect blue sky. There wasn't a sound to be heard save for the occasional bird calling and the whisper of the breeze.

The text was beginning to drift before his eyes as he wrote it again and again. This was certainly no easy task. Linear time simply wasn't adequate. He was wired, on a trip to the end of the nervous system, to the end of the Invisible Environment. There is no guide no voice no word. Walled in by oscillographs of the past the crew plot a precarious course in dead space of random topographies. Infra-red TV screens, exposed nerve ends, phosphorescent comics, roentgen films & tapes of fictitious events, wind-tunnels of gossip, rigged history. He was cruising now, exploring uncharted avenues and alleyways, both literal and metaphorical, a cosmonaut of inner space.

Fuck chronology
Fuck sequentiality
Fuck linearity
Fuck the time-space continuum
Finally, this is working
Finally, this is life
This is like a slap in the face
This is like an amputation

like death, Tim gathered together the papers. The end was close now.

This is like a slap in the face
This is like an amputation

***

***

It was just another day – no easy task – a writer office, the same as any other. I certainly don't believe one chooses his desk. He had spent the last three to be a writer – I shan't say 'become' – hours trying desperately to compile his writer, because the word has latest report based on a series of site implications of evolution. That isn't to visit out-of-town shopping – say that a writer doesn't evolve – developments ahead of Friday's grow – writing requires a great deal of deadlines – but it was proving nigh on practice... commitment impossible. For a start, the building doesn't start as something else – a poor state of repair – and them slowly turn into a writer.

It was just another day – no easy task – a writer office, the same as any other. I certainly don't believe one 'chooses' his desk. He had spent the last three to be a writer – I shan't say 'become' – hours trying desperately to compile his writer, because the word has latest report based on a series of site implications of evolution. That isn't to visit out-of-town shopping – say that a writer doesn't evolve – developments ahead of Friday's grow – writing requires a great deal of deadline – but it was proving nigh on practice... commitment impossible. For a start, the buildings doesn't start as something else – a poor state of repair – and them slowly turn into a writer.

No, surveys had uncovered a number of writers, starts out as a writer, and significant structural flaws which were over time develop – practice bad news all round. The trouble was experience.

No, surveys had uncovered a number of writers, starts out as a writer, and significant structural flaws which were over time develop – practice bad news all round. The trouble was experience.

"Well, so one would find these modern prefabricated hopes, and I'm quite certain that my monstrosities

"Well, so one would find these modern prefabricated hopes, and I'm composed of concrete – own output –

quite certain that my monstrosities composed of concrete – own output – almost infinite – corrugated iron, better than it was fifteen years ago."

"While he has most – it was a compulsion. Information he required to hand, same as it is now. His notes were a little patchy – in the hands of The Plagiarist – but today my compulsion regarding some of the sites had been tired, as he had compelled to pursue other things..."

Conducting the surveys – that said, he screen for what seemed like hours. He didn't really find buildings in the clock on his Microsoft ® all that inspiring. He had been surveying – a calling for staring at the screen for hours. There – him – but then, to his mind, no point calling a passion. Surveying for the sake of it, to produce screes of job – even inferior prose – pragmatic approach to factual data later – he was a writer with a grasp of figures and certain scientific conscience and also a burning desire – concepts regarding the deterioration to change things – concrete, the weakening of iron – it was his objective to write the girders, the flammability of a certain world.

weakening of iron – it was his objective to write the girders, the flammability of a world, almost infinite, is better than it was."

"While he has most – it was a compulsion. Information he required to hand, same as it is now. His notes were a little patchy – in the hands of The Plagiarist – but today my compulsion regarding some of the sites had been tired, as he had compelled to pursue other things..."

Conducting the surveys – that said, he screen for what seemed like hours. He didn't really find buildings in the clock on his Microsoft ® all that inspiring. He had been surveying – a calling for staring at the screen for hours. There – him – but then, to his mind, no point calling a passion. Surveying for the sake of it, to produce screes of job – even inferior prose – pragmatic approach to factual data later – he was a writer with a grasp of figures and certain scientific conscience and also a burning desire – concepts regarding the deterioration to change things – concrete, the weakening of iron – it was his objective to write the girders, the flammability of a certain world.

*** ***

Exhausted following yet another interminably long and exhausting day at the office – end to end telephone calls and report-writing, Tim was in a daze of fatigue. He knew he should go home and get some rest, spend some quality time with Amy. But no, he felt he needed a temporary step out of life, if only for a few hours. And so he elected to leave his car at the office and get the train home – after hitting the pub for a couple or three first.

Tim sat and rubbed his eyes with his thumb and forefinger. His skin felt rough and dry, his eyes sensitive and watery. He was exhausted, and this was reflected in his sallow appearance. Then he picked up his coat and made his way out of the office.

Evening was starting to descend outside. It had been a long and arduous day, and summer was beginning to draw to a close now. The season was not yet far enough advanced for the first shades of Autumn to colour either the leaves or the sky, however, and there was still a warmth in the air. Nevertheless, he dug his hands into his pockets as he made his way down the street, hunching his shoulders slightly as he walked.

Exhausted following yet another interminably long and exhausting day of writing and revision that left his fingers aching and his back stiff, Ant was in a daze of fatigue. He knew he should call it a night, get some rest, revel in the completion of his manuscript. But no, he felt he needed a temporary step out of life, if only for a few hours. And so he elected to take a walk, get some fresh and then rest – after hitting the pub for a couple or three first.

Tone sat and rubbed his eyes with his thumb and forefinger. His skin felt rough and dry, his eyes sensitive and watery. He was exhausted, and this was reflected in his sallow appearance. Then he picked up his coat and made his way out of the house.

Evening was starting to descend outside. It had been a long and arduous day, and summer was beginning to draw to a close now. The season was not yet far enough advanced for the first shades of Autumn to colour either the leaves or the sky, however, and there was still a warmth in the air. Nevertheless, he dug his hands into his pockets as he made his way down the street, hunching his shoulders slightly as he walked.

It had been just another day at the office, the same as any other. Most buildings were unremarkably uninspiring to assess and nothing like those in Nikolaus Pevsner's seminal tome *An Outline of European Architecture*. Not that it had been a passion for architecture or construction that had led him down the career path on which he found himself: no, that had been down to what he was able to do, what constituted a solid long-term career and the prospect of a decent salary if he worked hard and made his charter.

His thoughts turned to his career as he made his way to the pub. He wasn't entirely certain which one to stop in at. After all, he wasn't meeting anyone, didn't have any deadlines or anywhere specific to be at any specific time, although he didn't want to be too late, and thought he should perhaps give Amy a call to let her know what he was doing.

But what was he doing? he thought to himself. Nothing now, that much was obvious. It was a man's prerogative to have a quiet pint after work, to clear his head. Better than taking out his frustrations on his partner. But long term? He wasn't sure if this was what he wanted, wasn't really sure what he wanted at all. In the

It's no easy task being a writer. Ant certainly didn't 'choose' to be a writer. *Writing chose him.* This thought stuck him as he walked down the street toward the pub. He was still in two minds as to precisely where to go. He wasn't meeting anyone, didn't have any deadlines or anywhere specific to be at any specific time. Although only just scraping a living as a writer, it beat the crap out his previous career as an administrator at the council, a job he'd fallen into by default and stuck out for longer than he'd planned, than was good for his sanity.

His thoughts turned to his career as he made his way past the hospital. He really didn't fancy the mediocre draughts on offer at The West End, and the Grapes wouldn't yet be open. And so he found himself once again heading down Glossop Road, avoiding the Wetherspoons and other trendy bars in favour of the Frog and Parrot, where he knew he could at least get a decent pint, and the jukebox wasn't usually too obtrusive. He knew he needed some kind of a break: the odd-jobbing was, he felt, the literary equivalent of a tramp routing through bins for fag ends, but nevertheless substantially more dignified than grinding out the same shit to someone else's beat on the 9-5, where fulfilment

back of his mind, he felt unfulfilled.

He arrived at a pub he hadn't tried before. It looked ok, reasonably quiet and some hand pumps on the bar. As summer was over, it was time to switch from lager back to bitter. He walked in and walked up to the bar, took a quick look around before the barmaid, a pretty, young-looking blonde, noticed him and came over.

"Hello there," she said with a smile, "what can I get you?"

Tim hesitated as he studied the selection of ales on the pumps.

"Er, a pint of Moonshine, please," he replied hesitantly.

She pulled the pint. It had a rather large head, but he wasn't about to make a fuss. He picked up the glass and turned to look around once more. There weren't many others in. A trendy, student-looking couple, seated in one corner, were huddled close and laughing. A fat, middle-aged man in jacket and jeans was seated at one end of the bar, and in the farthest corner, a skinny looking guy in black Levi's and a well-worn black leather jacket was positioned, with various objects strewn about the table before him as he scribbled into a notepad, glancing up furtively from time to time. *Weirdo.*

Tim seated himself in another corner, from which he could see the

simply wasn't an option.

He arrived at the pub and walked on in. It was reasonably quiet, and the pumps all had forward-facing tags, including some guest ales. He had a thirst only a beer could quench. He walked up to the bar, glancing around for available tables before the barmaid, a pretty, young-looking blonde, noticed him and came over.

"Hello there," she smiled, "what can I get you?"

Ant hesitated as he studied the selection of ales on the pumps.

"Er, a pint of Moonshine, please," he replied.

She pulled the pint. It had a rather large head, but she topped it up without being asked. He picked up the glass and turned to look around once more. There weren't many others in. A trendy, student-looking couple, seated in one corner, were huddled close and laughing. A fat, middle-aged man in jacket and jeans was seated at one end of the bar, and in the farthest corner, a skinny looking guy in a grey pinstripe suit and tie was positioned, a mobile phone on the table before him, at which he glanced furtively from time to time, as if doing so would make it ring. *Loser. Corporate slave.*

Tony seated himself in another corner, from which he could see the place in its entirety, before placing his pint toward the centre of the circular table and emptying the contents of his pockets onto the surface. It was a routine he had. He wasn't entirely sure why, or how it had evolved. Marking his territory, he supposed.

Mobile phone, pen, car keys, wallet. Granted, not the most sensible thing to leave on display, but it was uncomfortable in his back pocket, and besides, if it was in sight, he knew he'd not left it anywhere. It was a strange habit, his friends said, but so what?

He took a long draught down of his pint. The amber fluid was cool, lightly hoppy, refreshing. Then he picked up his phone and tried calling Amy. He had her on speed-dial. No reply. Where could she be? He pondered the possibilities for a moment. She wasn't one to go out without saying. Perhaps she was in the bath?

His attention skipped from one thing to another, entirely arbitrarily. He didn't really pay his thought processes any attention, they were simply a number of programs that ran in the background, constantly. All part of the machine. All part of the machine... he was a man-machine. He was also part of the corporate machine in his place of work. And a small cog in the

place in its entirety, before placing his pint toward the centre of the circular table and emptying the contents of his pockets onto the surface. It was a routine he had. He wasn't entirely sure why, or how it had evolved. Marking his territory, he supposed.

Mobile phone, pen, MP3 player, book, notepad. He always carried a pen and notepad, was always ready to scribble when something caught his eye. Didn't want to pass up on any potential material. He was a writer by compulsion, not choice.

He took a long draught down of his pint. The amber fluid was cool, lightly hoppy, refreshing. Then he picked up his book, a beaten copy of Leonard Cohen's *Beautiful Losers* and began to read. It was a book he loved, but found difficult to maintain focus on for long periods due to the density of the prose style and its curiously penned detail. His mind wandered, and his attention skipped from one thing to another, entirely arbitrarily. He didn't usually pay his thought processes any attention, they were simply a number of programs that ran in the background, constantly. All part of the machine. But here, he momentarily became attuned. His internal dialogue, the flow of thoughts and images and his immediate surroundings and his

machine that is society. He sipped from his pint and glanced at a girl who had just walked in. He couldn't help it: he was getting fidgety, playing with his mobile, making furtive calls without reply and constantly checking it, as though to do so would make it ring.

He clocked the weird bastard across the way, glancing round, pen hovering over his pad like a reporter poised for the story to break. Maybe it would, in his head. There was nothing to see here, after all. He looked haunted, desperate. But Tim felt no pity. The freak's presence and behaviour made him feel uncomfortable, nervous. He kept looking at him, too, which didn't help. He had a strange look in his eye, a hint of something fearful. Tim, too, felt an unease, and wasn't sure if it was the uncertainty over Amy's whereabouts or something about the stranger's presence. His stomach was taut as he glanced again at the girl at the bar, who was standing now, laughing, with a couple of friends, and back once again at the bloke who was looking around and writing.

He glanced at his watch, at his mobile – it refused to ring. He should have been pleased: he was thoroughly sick of that fucking ring-tone, but hadn't had time to change it. The girl

conscious attained a fleeting moment of synergy. He was also conscious of the suit across the way. He was getting fidgety, playing with his mobile, making furtive calls without reply and constantly checking it, as though to do so would make it ring. It pained him to admit it, but he saw aspects of himself in this uneasy looking waif of a man wrapped in the attire of business. He looked haunted, desperate, like he didn't belong, but wasn't sure exactly how to deal with it. Ant was aware of the suit frequently casting glances his way. He had a strange look in his eye, a hint of something fearful. He looked uncomfortable, nervous. The disquiet was feeding into Anthony, too. He felt something shudder through him. At that moment, he knew what he must do. The idea hit him like a freight train, and he began to scribble notes in his pad. He would fill in the gaps later, develop the expression in order to convey the anxiety, the pain and the anguish. The chronology, too, could be negotiated at a future juncture. But for now, he had to capture as much as he could, assimilating every detail of his surroundings, every last aroma in the air, every snippet of dialogue, every stitch in the nap of the cloth that formed the fabric of life, of the lives, that were going on around him. He was

was wearing a short denim skirt and had shapely legs, he thought. He checked his watch again. He drained the last of his pint. He checked his watch again.

His glass was empty. The night was young, and he didn't want to go home yet he had. Time for another...

not a participant, he was an observer, a recorder. There would come a time when it was necessary to run playback. But that time was not now. He glanced around: plenty of material here.

His glass was empty. The night was young, and he had work to do. Time for another...

www.ingramcontent.com/pod-product-compliance
Lightning Source LLC
Chambersburg PA
CBHW020328130626
46549CB00003B/1077